Charles Dudley Warner

The American Italy

Our Italy

Charles Dudley Warner

The American Italy
Our Italy

ISBN/EAN: 9783337237875

Printed in Europe, USA, Canada, Australia, Japan

Cover: Foto ©Andreas Hilbeck / pixelio.de

More available books at **www.hansebooks.com**

SANTA BARBARA.

THE AMERICAN ITALY

(OUR ITALY)

BY

CHARLES DUDLEY WARNER

AUTHOR OF "THEIR PILGRIMAGE" "STUDIES IN THE SOUTH AND WEST"
"A LITTLE JOURNEY IN THE WORLD" ETC.

WITH MANY ILLUSTRATIONS

LONDON
JAMES R. OSGOOD, McILVAINE & CO.
45 ALBEMARLE STREET
1892

CONTENTS.

ILLUSTRATIONS.

ILLUSTRATIONS.

OUR ITALY.

CHAPTER I

HOW OUR ITALY IS MADE.

THE traveller who descends into Italy by an Alpine pass never forgets the surprise and delight of the transition. In an hour he is whirled down the slopes from the region of eternal snow to the verdure of spring or the ripeness of summer. Suddenly—it may be at a turn in the road—winter is left behind; the plains of Lombardy are in view; the Lake of Como or Maggiore gleams below; there is a tree; there is an orchard; there is a garden; there is a villa overrun with vines; the singing of birds is heard; the air is gracious; the slopes are terraced, and covered with vineyards; great sheets of silver sheen in the landscape mark the growth of the olive; the dark green orchards of oranges and lemons are starred with gold; the lusty fig, always a temptation as of old, leans invitingly over the stone wall; everywhere are bloom and color under the blue sky; there are shrines by the way-side, chapels on the hill; one hears the melodious bells, the call of the vine-dressers, the laughter of girls.

1

The contrast is as great from the Indians of the Mojave Desert, two types of which are here given, to the vine-dressers of the Santa Ana Valley.

Italy is the land of the imagination, but the sensation on first beholding it from the northern heights, aside from its associations of romance and poetry, can be repeated in our own land by whoever will cross the burning desert of Colorado, or the savage wastes of the Mojave wilderness of stone and sage-brush, and come suddenly, as he must come by train, into the bloom of Southern California. Let us study a little the physical conditions.

The bay of San Diego is about three hundred miles east of San Francisco. The coast line runs southeast, but at Point Conception it turns sharply east, and then curves south-easterly about two hundred and fifty miles to the Mexican coast boundary, the extreme south-west limits of the United States, a few miles below San Diego. This coast, defined by these two limits, has a southern exposure on the sunniest of oceans. Off this coast, south of Point Conception, lies a chain of islands, curving in position in conformity with the shore, at a distance of twenty to seventy miles from the main-land. These islands are San Miguel, Santa Rosa, Santa Cruz, Anacapa, Santa Barbara, San Nicolas, Santa Catalina, San Clemente, and Los Coronados, which lie in Mexican waters. Between this chain of islands and the main-land is Santa Barbara Channel, flowing northward. The great ocean current from the north flows past Point Conception like a mill-race, and makes a suction, or a sort of eddy. It approaches nearer the coast in Lower California, where the return current,

which is much warmer, flows northward and westward
along the curving shore. The Santa Barbara Channel,
which may be called an arm of the Pacific, flows by

MOJAVE DESERT.

many a bold point and lovely bay, like those of San
Pedro, Redondo, and Santa Monica; but it has no se-
cure harbor, except the magnificent and unique bay of
San Diego.

The southern and western boundary of Southern
California is this mild Pacific sea, studded with rocky
and picturesque islands. The northern boundary of
this region is ranges of lofty mountains, from five
thousand to eleven thousand feet in height, some of
them always snow-clad, which run eastward from
Point Conception nearly to the Colorado Desert. They
are parts of the Sierra Nevada range, but they take

various names, Santa Ynes, San Gabriel, San Bernardino, and they are spoken of all together as the Sierra Madre. In the San Gabriel group, "Old Baldy" lifts its snow-peak over nine thousand feet, while the San Bernardino "Grayback" rises over eleven thousand feet

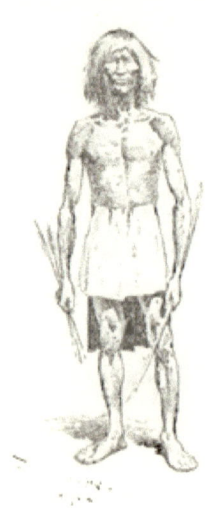

above the sea. Southward of this, running down into San Diego County, is the San Jacinto range, also snow-clad; and eastward the land falls rapidly away into the Salt Desert of the Colorado, in which is a depression about three hundred feet below the Pacific.

The Point Arguilles, which is above Point Conception, by the aid of the outlying islands, deflects the cold current from the north off the coast of Southern California, and the mountain ranges from Point Conception east divide the State of California into two climatic regions, the southern having more warmth, less rain and fog, milder winds, and less variation of daily temperature than the climate of Central California to the north.* Other striking climatic conditions are produced by the daily interaction of the Pacific Ocean and the Colorado Desert, infinitely diversified in minor particulars by the exceedingly broken character of the region—a jumble of bare mountains, fruitful foot-hills, and rich valleys. It would be

---

* For these and other observations upon physical and climatic conditions I am wholly indebted to Dr. P. C. Remondino and Mr. T. S. Van Dyke, of San Diego, both scientific and competent authorities.

only from a balloon that one could get an adequate idea of this strange land.

The United States has here, then, a unique corner of the earth, without its like in its own vast territory, and unparalleled, so far as I know, in the world. Shut off from sympathy with external conditions by the giant mountain ranges and the desert wastes, it has its own climate unaffected by cosmic changes. Except a tidal wave from Japan, nothing would seem to be able to affect or disturb it. The whole of Italy feels more or less the climatic variations of the rest of Europe. All our Atlantic coast, all our interior basin from Texas to Manitoba, is in climatic sympathy. Here is a region larger than New England which manufactures its own weather and refuses to import any other.

With considerable varieties of temperature according to elevation or protection from the ocean breeze, its climate is nearly, on the whole, as agreeable as that of the Hawaiian Islands, though pitched in a lower key, and with greater variations between day and night. The key to its peculiarity, aside from its southern exposure, is the Colorado Desert. That desert, waterless and treeless, is cool at night and intolerably hot in the daytime, sending up a vast column of hot air, which cannot escape eastward, for Arizona manufactures a like column. It flows high above the mountains westward till it strikes the Pacific and parts with its heat,

creating an immense vacuum which is filled by the
air from the coast flowing up the slope and over the
range, and plunging down 6000 feet into the desert.
"It is easy to understand," says Mr. Van Dyke, making
his observations from the summit of the Cuyamaca, in
San Diego County, 6500 feet above the sea-level, "how
land thus rising a mile or more in fifty or sixty miles,
rising away from the coast, and falling off abruptly a
mile deep into the driest and hottest of American deserts, could have a great variety of climates. . . . Only
ten miles away on the east the summers are the hottest,
and only sixty miles on the west the coolest known in
the United States (except on this coast), and between
them is every combination that mountains and valleys
can produce. And it is easy to see whence comes the
sea-breeze, the glory of the California summer. It is
passing us here, a gentle breeze of six or eight miles
an hour. It is flowing over this great ridge directly
into the basin of the Colorado Desert, 6000 feet deep,
where the temperature is probably 120°, and perhaps
higher. For many leagues each side of us this current is thus flowing at the same speed, and is probably half a mile or more in depth. About sundown,
when the air on the desert cools and descends, the
current will change and come the other way, and flood
these western slopes with an air as pure as that of the
Sahara and nearly as dry.

"The air, heated on the western slopes by the sea,
would by rising produce considerable suction, which
could be filled only from the sea, but that alone would
not make the sea-breeze as dry as it is. The principal
suction is caused by the rising of heated air from the
great desert. . . . On the top of old Grayback (in San

BIRD'S EYE VIEW OF RIVERSIDE.

Bernardino) one can feel it [this breeze] setting westward, while in the cañons, 6000 feet below, it is blowing eastward. . . . All over Southern California the
conditions of this breeze are about the same, the great
Mojave Desert and the valley of the San Joaquin
above operating in the same way, assisted by interior

plains and slopes. Hence these deserts, that at first seem to be a disadvantage to the land, are the great conditions of its climate, and are of far more value than if they were like the prairies of Illinois. Fortunately they will remain deserts forever. Some parts will in time be reclaimed by the waters of the Colorado River, but wet spots of a few hundred thousand acres would be too trifling to affect general results, for millions of acres of burning desert would forever defy all attempts at irrigation or settlement."

This desert-born breeze explains a seeming anomaly in regard to the humidity of this coast. I have noticed on the sea-shore that salt does not become damp on the table, that the Portuguese fishermen on Point Loma are drying their fish on the shore, and that while the hydrometer gives a humidity as high as seventy-four, and higher at times, and fog may prevail for three or four days continuously, the fog is rather "dry," and the general impression is that of a dry instead of the damp and chilling atmosphere such as exists in foggy times on the Atlantic coast.

" From the study of the origin of this breeze we see," says Mr. Van Dyke, "why it is that a wind coming from the broad Pacific should be drier than the dry land-breezes of the Atlantic States, causing no damp walls, swelling doors, or rusting guns, and even on the coast drying up, without salt or soda, meat cut in strips an inch thick and fish much thicker."

At times on the coast the air contains plenty of moisture, but with the rising of this breeze the moisture decreases instead of increases. It should be said also that this constantly returning current of air is

always pure, coming in contact nowhere with marshy
or malarious influences nor any agency injurious to
health.   Its character causes the whole coast from
Santa Barbara to San Diego to be an agreeable place
of residence or resort summer and winter, while its
daily inflowing tempers the heat of the far inland valleys to a delightful atmosphere in the shade even in
midsummer, while cool nights are everywhere the rule.
The greatest surprise of the traveller is that a region
which is in perpetual bloom and fruitage, where semi-
tropical fruits mature in perfection, and the most
delicate flowers dazzle the eye with color the winter
through, should have on the whole a low temperature,
a climate never enervating, and one requiring a dress
of woollen in every month.

CHAPTER II

WINTER as we understand it east of the Rockies does not exist. I scarcely know how to divide the seasons. There are at most but three. Spring may be said to begin with December and end in April; summer, with May (whose days, however, are often cooler than those of January), and end with September; while October and November are a mild autumn, when nature takes a partial rest, and the leaves of the deciduous trees are gone. But how shall we classify a climate in which the strawberry (none yet in my experience equal to the Eastern berry) may be eaten in every month of the year, and ripe figs may be picked from July to March? What shall I say of a frost (an affair of only an hour just before sunrise) which is hardly anywhere severe enough to disturb the delicate heliotrope, and even in the deepest valleys where it may chill the orange, will respect the bloom of that fruit on contiguous ground fifty or a hundred feet higher? We boast about many things in the United States, about our blizzards and our cyclones, our inundations and our areas of low pressure, our hottest and our coldest places in the world, but what can we say for this little corner which is practically frostless, and yet never had a sunstroke, knows nothing of thunder-storms and lightning, never experienced a cyclone,

which is so warm that the year round one is tempted
to live out-of-doors, and so cold that woollen garments
are never uncomfortable? Nature here, in this protected and petted area, has the knack of being genial
without being enervating, of being stimulating without "bracing" a person into the tomb. I think it con-
ducive to equanimity of spirit and to longevity to sit
in an orange grove and eat the fruit and inhale the
fragrance of it while gazing upon a snow-mountain.

SCENE IN SAN BERNARDINO.

This southward-facing portion of California is irrigated by many streams of pure water rapidly falling
from the mountains to the sea. The more important
are the Santa Clara, the Los Angeles and San Gabriel,
the Santa Ana, the Santa Margarita, the San Luis
Rey, the San Bernardo, the San Diego, and, on the
Mexican border, the Tia Juana. Many of them go
dry or flow underground in the summer months (or,
as the Californians say, the bed of the river gets on
top), but most of them can be used for artificial irriga-

tion. In the lowlands water is sufficiently near the surface to moisten the soil, which is broken and cultivated; in most regions good wells are reached at a small depth, in others artesian-wells spout up abundance of water, and considerable portions of the regions best known for fruit are watered by irrigating ditches and pipes supplied by ample reservoirs in the mountains. From natural rainfall and the sea moisture the mesas and hills, which look arid before ploughing, produce large crops of grain when cultivated after the annual rains, without artificial watering.

Southern California has been slowly understood even by its occupants, who have wearied the world with boasting of its productiveness. Originally it was a vast cattle and sheep ranch. It was supposed that the land was worthless except for grazing. Held in princely ranches of twenty, fifty, one hundred thousand acres, in some cases areas larger than German principalities, tens of thousands of cattle roamed along the watercourses and over the mesas, vast flocks of sheep cropped close the grass and trod the soil into hard-pan. The owners exchanged cattle and sheep for corn, grain, and garden vegetables; they had no faith that they could grow cereals, and it was too much trouble to procure water for a garden or a fruit orchard. It was the firm belief that most of the rolling mesa land was unfit for cultivation, and that neither forest nor fruit trees would grow without irrigation. Between Los Angeles and Redondo Beach is a ranch of 35,000 acres. Seventeen years ago it was owned by a Scotchman, who used the whole of it as a sheep ranch. In selling it to the present owner he warned him not to waste time by attempting to farm it; he

SCENES IN MONTECITO AND LOS ANGELES.

himself raised no fruit or vegetables, planted no trees, and bought all his corn, wheat, and barley. The purchaser, however, began to experiment. He planted trees and set out orchards which grew, and in a couple of years he wrote to the former owner that he had 8000 acres in fine wheat. To say it in a word, there is scarcely an acre of the tract which is not highly productive in barley, wheat, corn, potatoes, while considerable parts of it are especially adapted to the English walnut and to the citrus fruits.

On this route to the sea the road is lined with gardens. Nothing could be more unpromising in appearance than this soil before it is ploughed and pulverized by the cultivator. It looks like a barren waste. We passed a tract that was offered three years ago for twelve dollars an acre. Some of it now is rented to Chinamen at thirty dollars an acre; and I saw one field of two acres off which a Chinaman has sold in one season $750 worth of cabbages.

The truth is that almost all the land is wonderfully productive if intelligently handled. The low ground has water so near the surface that the pulverized soil will draw up sufficient moisture for the crops; the mesa, if sown and cultivated after the annual rains, matures grain and corn, and sustains vines and fruit-trees. It is singular that the first settlers should never have discovered this productiveness. When it became apparent—that is, productiveness without artificial watering — there spread abroad a notion that irrigation generally was not needed. We shall have occasion to speak of this more in detail, and I will now only say, on good authority, that while cultivation, not to keep down the weeds only, but to keep the soil stirred and

prevent its baking, is the prime necessity for almost all
land in Southern California, there are portions where
irrigation is always necessary, and there is no spot
where the yield of fruit or grain will not be quadru-
pled by judicious irrigation. There are places where
irrigation is excessive and harmful both to the quality and quantity of oranges and grapes.

The history of the extension of cultivation in the
last twenty and especially in the past ten years from
the foot-hills of the Sierra Madre in Los Angeles and
San Bernardino counties southward to San Diego is
very curious. Experiments were timidly tried. Every
acre of sand and sage-bush reclaimed southward was
supposed to be the last capable of profitable farming
or fruit-growing. It is unsafe now to say of any land
that has not been tried that it is not good. In every
valley and on every hill-side, on the mesas and in the
sunny nooks in the mountains, nearly anything will
grow, and the application of water produces marvellous results. From San Bernardino and Redlands,
Riverside, Pomona, Ontario, Santa Anita, San Gabriel,
Pasadena, all the way to Los Angeles, is almost a continuous fruit garden, the green areas only empha-
sized by wastes yet unreclaimed; a land of charming
cottages, thriving towns, hospitable to the fruit of
every clime; a land of perpetual sun and ever-flowing
breeze, looked down on by purple mountain ranges
tipped here and there with enduring snow. And what
is in progress here will be seen before long in almost
every part of this wonderful land, for conditions of
soil and climate are essentially everywhere the same,
and capital is finding out how to store in and bring
from the fastnesses of the mountains rivers of clear

FAN-PALM, LOS ANGELES.

water taken at such elevations that the whole arable surface can be irrigated. The development of the country has only just begun.

If the reader will look upon the map of California he will see that the eight counties that form Southern California—San Luis Obispo, Santa Barbara, Ventura, Kern, Los Angeles, San Bernardino, Orange, and San Diego—appear very mountainous. He will also notice that the eastern slopes of San Bernardino and San Diego are deserts. But this is an immense area. San Diego County alone is as large as Massachusetts, Con-

necticut, and Rhode Island combined, and the amount
of arable land in the valleys, on the foot-hills, on the
rolling mesas, is enormous, and capable of sustaining a
dense population, for its fertility and its yield to the
acre under cultivation are incomparable. The reader
will also notice another thing. With the railroads
now built and certain to be built through all this diversified region, round from the Santa Barbara Mountains to the San Bernardino, the San Jacinto, and

YUCCA-PALM, SANTA BARBARA.

down to Cuyamaca, a ride of an hour or two hours
brings one to some point on the 250 miles of sea-coast
—a sea-coast genial, inviting in winter and summer,
never harsh, and rarely tempestuous like the Atlantic
shore.

Here is our Mediterranean! Here is our Italy! It
is a Mediterranean without marshes and without malaria, and it does not at all resemble the Mexican Gulf,
which we have sometimes tried to fancy was like the
classic sea that laves Africa and Europe. Nor is this
region Italian in appearance, though now and then
some bay with its purple hills running to the blue sea,
its surrounding mesas and cañons blooming in semi-
tropical luxuriance, some conjunction of shore and
mountain, some golden color, some white light and
sharply defined shadows, some refinement of lines,
some poetic tints in violet and ashy ranges, some
ultramarine in the sea, or delicate blue in the sky, will
remind the traveller of more than one place of beauty
in Southern Italy and Sicily. It is a Mediterranean
with a more equable climate, warmer winters and
cooler summers, than the North Mediterranean shore
can offer; it is an Italy whose mountains and valleys
give almost every variety of elevation and temperature.

But it is our commercial Mediterranean. The time
is not distant when this corner of the United States
will produce in abundance, and year after year without failure, all the fruits and nuts which for a thousand years the civilized world of Europe has looked to
the Mediterranean to supply. We shall not need any
more to send over the Atlantic for raisins, English
walnuts, almonds, figs, olives, prunes, oranges, lemons,
limes, and a variety of other things which we know

commercially as Mediterranean products. We have all this luxury and wealth at our doors, within our limits. The orange and the lemon we shall still bring from many places; the date and the pineapple and the banana will never grow here except as illustrations of the climate, but it is difficult to name any fruit of the temperate and semi-tropic zones that Southern California cannot be relied on to produce, from the guava to the peach.

It will need further experiment to determine what are the more profitable products of this soil, and it will take longer experience to cultivate them and send them to market in perfection. The pomegranate and the apple thrive side by side, but the apple is not good here unless it is grown at an elevation where frost is certain and occasional snow may be expected. There is no longer any doubt about the peach, the nectarine, the pear, the grape, the orange, the lemon, the apricot. and so on; but I believe that the greatest profit will be in the products that cannot be grown elsewhere in the United States—the products to which we have long given the name of Mediterranean—the olive, the fig, the raisin, the hard and soft shell almond, and the walnut. The orange will of course be a staple, and constantly improve its reputation as better varieties are raised, and the right amount of irrigation to produce the finest and sweetest is ascertained.

It is still a wonder that a land in which there was no indigenous product of value, or to which cultivation could give value, should be so hospitable to every sort of tree, shrub, root, grain, and flower that can be brought here from any zone and temperature, and that many of these foreigners to the soil grow here

with a vigor and productiveness surpassing those in
their native land. This bewildering adaptability has
misled many into unprofitable experiments, and the
very rapidity of growth has been a disadvantage.
The land has been advertised by its monstrous vegetable productions, which are not fit to eat, and but
testify to the fertility of the soil; and the reputation
of its fruits, both deciduous and citrus, has suffered
by specimens sent to Eastern markets whose sole rec-
ommendation was size. Even in the vineyards and
orange orchards quality has been sacrificed to quantity. Nature here responds generously to every encouragement, but it cannot be forced without taking
its revenge in the return of inferior quality. It is just
as true of Southern California as of any other land,
that hard work and sagacity and experience are necessary to successful horticulture and agriculture, but
it is undeniably true that the same amount of well-
directed industry upon a much smaller area of land
will produce more return than in almost any other
section of the United States. Sensible people do not
any longer pay much attention to those tempting little
arithmetical sums by which it is demonstrated that
paying so much for ten acres of barren land, and so
much for planting it with vines or oranges, the income in three years will be a competence to the in-
vestor and his family. People do not spend much
time now in gaping over abnormal vegetables, or try-
ing to convince themselves that wines of every known
variety and flavor can be produced within the limits
of one flat and well-watered field. Few now expect to
make a fortune by cutting arid land up into twenty-
feet lots, but notwithstanding the extravagance of re-

cent speculation, the value of arable land has steadily
appreciated, and is not likely to recede, for the return
from it, either in fruits, vegetables, or grain, is demonstrated to be beyond the experience of farming elsewhere.

Land cannot be called dear at one hundred or one
thousand dollars an acre if the annual return from it
is fifty or five hundred dollars. The climate is most
agreeable the year through. There are no unpleasant
months, and few unpleasant days. The eucalyptus
grows so fast that the trimmings from the trees of a
small grove or highway avenue will in four or five
years furnish a family with its firewood. The strong,
fattening alfalfa gives three, four, five, and even six
harvests a year. Nature needs little rest, and, with
the encouragement of water and fertilizers, apparently
none. But all this prodigality and easiness of life de-
tracts a little from ambition. The lesson has been
slowly learned, but it is now pretty well conned, that
hard work is as necessary here as elsewhere to thrift
and independence. The difference between this and
many other parts of our land is that nature seems to
work with a man, and not against him.

CHAPTER III.

SOUTHERN CALIFORNIA has rapidly passed through
varied experiences, and has not yet had a fair chance
to show the world what it is. It had its period of romance, of pastoral life, of lawless adventure, of crazy
speculation, all within a hundred years, and it is just
now entering upon its period of solid, civilized development. A certain light of romance is cast upon this
coast by the Spanish voyagers of the sixteenth century, but its history begins with the establishment of
the chain of Franciscan missions, the first of which
was founded by the great Father Junipero Serra at
San Diego in 1769. The fathers brought with them
the vine and the olive, reduced the savage Indians to
industrial pursuits, and opened the way for that ran-
chero and adobe civilization which, down to the coming of the American, in about 1840, made in this region the most picturesque life that our continent has
ever seen. Following this is a period of desperado
adventure and revolution, of pioneer State-building;
and then the advent of the restless, the cranky, the
invalid, the fanatic, from every other State in the
Union. The first experimenters in making homes
seem to have fancied that they had come to a ready-
made elysium—the idle man's heaven. They seem to

have brought with them little knowledge of agriculture or horticulture, were ignorant of the conditions of
success in this soil and climate, and left behind the
good industrial maxims of the East. The result was
a period of chance experiment, one in which extravagant expectation and boasting to some extent took the
place of industry. The imagination was heated by
the novelty of such varied and rapid productiveness.
Men's minds were inflamed by the apparently limitless
possibilities. The invalid and the speculator throng-
ed the transcontinental roads leading thither. In this
condition the frenzy of 1886–87 was inevitable. I saw
something of it in the winter of 1887. The scenes
then daily and commonplace now read like the wild-
est freaks of the imagination.

The bubble collapsed as suddenly as it expanded.
Many were ruined, and left the country. More were
merely ruined in their great expectations. The speculation was in town lots. When it subsided it left
the climate as it was, the fertility as it was, and the
value of arable land not reduced. Marvellous as the
boom was, I think the present recuperation is still
more wonderful. In 1890, to be sure, I miss the
bustle of the cities, and the creation of towns in a
week under the hammer of the auctioneer. But in all
the cities, and most of the villages, there has been
growth in substantial buildings, and in the necessities
of civic life—good sewerage, water supply, and general organization; while the country, as the acreage
of vines and oranges, wheat and barley, grain and
corn, and the shipments by rail testify, has improved
more than at any other period, and commerce is beginning to feel the impulse of a genuine prosperity.

based upon the intelligent cultivation of the ground.
School-houses have multiplied; libraries have been
founded; many "boom" hotels, built in order to sell
city lots in the sage-brush, have been turned into
schools and colleges.

There is immense rivalry between different sections. Every Californian thinks that the spot where
his house stands enjoys the best climate and is the
most fertile in the world; and while you are with him
you think he is justified in his opinion; for this rivalry is generally a wholesome one, backed by industry.
I do not mean to say that the habit of tall talk is altogether lost. Whatever one sees he is asked to believe is the largest and best in the world. The gentleman of the whip who showed us some of the finest
places in Los Angeles—places that in their wealth of
flowers and semi-tropical gardens would rouse the
enthusiasm of the most jaded traveller—was asked
whether there were any finer in the city. "Finer?
Hundreds of them;" and then, meditatively and re-
gretfully, "I should not dare to show you the best."
The semi-ecclesiastical custodian of the old adobe mission of San Gabriel explained to us the twenty por-
traits of apostles on the walls, all done by Murillo.
As they had got out of repair, he had them all re-
painted by the best artist. "That one," he said, simply, "cost ten dollars. It often costs more to repaint
a picture than to buy an original."

The temporary evils in the train of the "boom"
are fast disappearing. I was told that I should find
the country stagnant. Trade, it is true, is only slowly
coming in, real-estate deals are sleeping, but in all
avenues of solid prosperity and productiveness the

AVENUE LOS ANGELES.

country is the reverse of stagnant. Another misapprehension this visit is correcting. I was told not to visit Southern California at this season on account of the heat. But I have no experience of a more delightful summer climate than this, especially on or near the coast.

In secluded valleys in the interior the thermometer rises in the daytime to 85°, 90°, and occasionally 100°, but I have found no place in them where there was not daily a refreshing breeze from the ocean, where the dryness of the air did not make the heat seem much less than it was, and where the nights were not agreeably cool. My belief is that the summer climate of Southern California is as desirable for pleasure-seekers, for invalids, for workmen, as its winter climate. It seems to me that a coast temperature 60° to 75°, stimulating, without harshness or dampness, is about the perfection of summer weather. It should be said, however, that there are secluded valleys which become very hot in the daytime in midsummer, and intolerably dusty. The dust is the great annoyance everywhere. It gives the whole landscape an ashy tint, like some of our Eastern fields and waysides in a dry August. The verdure and the wild flowers of the rainy season disappear entirely. There is, however, some picturesque compensation for this dust and lack of green. The mountains and hills and great plains take on wonderful hues of brown, yellow, and red.

I write this paragraph in a high chamber in the Hotel del Coronado, on the great and fertile beach in front of San Diego. It is the 2d of June. Looking southward, I see the great expanse of the Pacific

Ocean, sparkling in the sun as blue as the waters at
Amalfi. A low surf beats along the miles and miles
of white sand continually, with the impetus of far-off
seas and trade-winds, as it has beaten for thousands
of years, with one unending roar and swish, and
occasional shocks of sound as if of distant thunder
on the shore. Yonder, to the right, Point Loma
stretches its sharp and rocky promontory into the
ocean, purple in the sun, bearing a light-house on its
highest elevation. From this signal, bending in a
perfect crescent, with a silver rim, the shore sweeps
around twenty-five miles to another promontory running down beyond Tia Juana to the Point of Rocks,
in Mexican territory. Directly in front — they say
eighteen miles away, I think five sometimes, and
sometimes a hundred — lie the islands of Coronado,
named, I suppose, from the old Spanish adventurer
Vasques de Coronado, huge bulks of beautiful red
sandstone, uninhabited and barren, becalmed there in
the changing blue of sky and sea, like enormous
mastless galleons, like degraded icebergs, like Capri
and Ischia. They say that they are stationary. I
only know that when I walk along the shore towards
Point Loma they seem to follow, until they lie opposite the harbor entrance, which is close by the promontory; and that when I return, they recede and go
away towards Mexico, to which they belong. Sometimes, as seen from the beach, owing to the difference in the humidity of the strata of air over the
ocean, they seem smaller at the bottom than at the
top. Occasionally they come quite near, as do the
sea-lions and the gulls, and again they almost fade
out of the horizon in a violet light. This morning

IN THE GARDEN AT SANTA BARBARA MISSION.

they stand away, and the fleet of white-sailed fishing-
boats from the Portuguese hamlet of La Playa, within the harbor entrance, which is dancing off Point
Loma, will have a long sail if they pursue the barra-
cuda to those shadowy rocks.

We crossed the bay the other day, and drove up
a wild road to the height of the promontory, and
along its narrow ridge to the light-house. This site
commands one of the most remarkable views in the
accessible civilized world, one of the three or four
really great prospects which the traveller can recall,
astonishing in its immensity, interesting in its peculiar details. The general features are the great ocean,
blue, flecked with sparkling, breaking wavelets, and
the wide, curving coast-line, rising into mesas, foot-
hills, ranges on ranges of mountains, the faintly seen
snow-peaks of San Bernardino and San Jacinto to
the Cuyamaca and the flat top of Table Mountain in
Mexico. Directly under us on one side are the fields
of kelp, where the whales come to feed in winter;
and on the other is a point of sand on Coronado
Beach, where a flock of pelicans have assembled after
their day's fishing, in which occupation they are the
rivals of the Portuguese. The perfect crescent of
the ocean beach is seen, the singular formation of
North and South Coronado Beach, the entrance to
the harbor along Point Loma, and the spacious inner
bay, on which lie San Diego and National City, with
lowlands and heights outside sprinkled with houses,
gardens, orchards, and vineyards. The near hills
about this harbor are varied in form and poetic in
color, one of them, the conical San Miguel, constantly recalling Vesuvius. Indeed, the near view, in

3

color, vegetation, and forms of hills and extent of
arable land, suggests that of Naples, though on anal-
ysis it does not resemble it. If San Diego had half
a million of people it would be more like it; but the
Naples view is limited, while this stretches away to
the great mountains that overlook the Colorado Desert. It is certainly one of the loveliest prospects in
the world, and worth long travel to see.

Standing upon this point of view, I am reminded
again of the striking contrasts and contiguous different climates on the coast. In the north, of course not
visible from here, is Mount Whitney, on the borders
of Inyo County and of the State of Nevada, 15,086
feet above the sea, the highest peak in the United
States, excluding Alaska. South of it is Grayback, in
the San Bernardino range, 11,000 feet in altitude, the
highest point above its base in the United States.
While south of that is the depression in the Colorado Desert in San Diego County, about three hundred feet below the level of the Pacific Ocean, the
lowest land in the United States. These three exceptional points can be said to be almost in sight of
each other.

I have insisted so much upon the Mediterranean
character of this region that it is necessary to emphasize the contrasts also. Reserving details and
comments on different localities as to the commercial
value of products and climatic conditions, I will make
some general observations. I am convinced that the
fig can not only be grown here in sufficient quantity
to supply our markets, but of the best quality. The
same may be said of the English walnut. This clean
and handsome tree thrives wonderfully in large areas,

SCENE AT PASADENA.

and has no enemies. The olive culture is in its infancy, but I have never tasted better oil than that produced at Santa Barbara and on San Diego Bay. Specimens of the pickled olive are delicious, and when the best varieties are generally grown, and the best method of curing is adopted, it will be in great demand, not as a mere relish, but as food. The raisin is produced in all the valleys of Southern California, and in great quantities in the hot valley of San Joaquin, beyond the Sierra Madre range. The best Malaga raisins, which have the reputation of being the best in the world, may never come to our market, but I have never eaten a better raisin for size, flavor, and thinness of skin than those raised in the El Cajon Valley, which is watered by the great flume which taps a reservoir in the Cuyamaca Mountains, and supplies San Diego. But the quality of the raisin in California will be improved by experience in cultivation and handling.

The contrast with the Mediterranean region—I refer to the western basin—is in climate. There is hardly any point along the French and Italian coast that is not subject to great and sudden changes, caused by the north wind, which has many names, or in the extreme southern peninsula and islands by the sirocco. There are few points that are not reached by malaria, and in many resorts—and some of them most sunny and agreeable to the invalid—the deadliest fevers always lie in wait. There is great contrast between summer and winter, and exceeding variability in the same month. This variability is the parent of many diseases of the lungs, the bowels, and the liver. It is demonstrated now by long-continued observa-

tions that dampness and cold are not so inimical to
health as variability.

The Southern California climate is an anomaly. It
has been the subject of a good deal of wonder and a
good deal of boasting, but it is worthy of more scientific study than it has yet received. Its distinguishing
feature I take to be its equability. The temperature
the year through is lower than I had supposed, and
the contrast is not great between the summer and the
winter months. The same clothing is appropriate,
speaking generally, for the whole year. In all seasons, including the rainy days of the winter months,
sunshine is the rule. The variation of temperature
between day and night is considerable, but if the new-
comer exercises a little care, he will not be unpleas-
antly affected by it. There are coast fogs, but these
are not chilling and raw. Why it is that with the
hydrometer showing a considerable humidity in the
air the general effect of the climate is that of dryness,
scientists must explain. The constant exchange of
desert airs with the ocean air may account for the
anomaly, and the actual dryness of the soil, even on
the coast, is put forward as another explanation.
Those who come from heated rooms on the Atlantic
may find the winters cooler than they expect, and
those used to the heated terms of the Mississippi Valley and the East will be surprised at the cool and sa-
lubrious summers. A land without high winds or
thunder-storms may fairly be said to have a unique
climate.

I suppose it is the equability and not conditions
of dampness or dryness that renders this region so re-
markably exempt from epidemics and endemic dis-

cases. The diseases of children prevalent elsewhere
are unknown here; they cut their teeth without risk,
and *cholera infantum* never visits them. Diseases of
the bowels are practically unknown. There is no
malaria, whatever that may be, and consequently an

LIVE-OAK NEAR LOS ANGELES

absence of those various fevers and other disorders
which are attributed to malarial conditions. Renal
diseases are also wanting; disorders of the liver and
kidneys, and Bright's disease, gout, and rheumatism,
are not native. The climate in its effect is stimulating, but at the same time soothing to the nerves,
so that if "nervous prostration" is wanted, it must

be brought here, and cannot be relied on to continue
long. These facts are derived from medical practice
with the native Indian and Mexican population. Dr.
Remondino, to whom I have before referred, has made
the subject a study for eighteen years, and later I
shall offer some of the results of his observations
upon longevity. It is beyond my province to vent-
ure any suggestion upon the effect of the climate
upon deep-seated diseases, especially of the respiratory organs, of invalids who come here for health. I
only know that we meet daily and constantly so
many persons in fair health who say that it is impossible for them to live elsewhere that the impression is produced that a considerable proportion of
the immigrant population was invalid. There are,
however, two suggestions that should be made. Care
is needed in acclimation to a climate that differs
from any previous experience; and the locality that
will suit any invalid can only be determined by personal experience. If the coast does not suit him, he
may be benefited in a protected valley, or he may be
improved on the foot-hills, or on an elevated mesa, or
on a high mountain elevation.

One thing may be regarded as settled. Whatever
the sensibility or the peculiarity of invalidism, the
equable climate is exceedingly favorable to the smooth
working of the great organic functions of respiration,
digestion, and circulation.

It is a pity to give this chapter a medical tone.
One need not be an invalid to come here and appreciate the graciousness of the air; the color of the
landscape, which is wanting in our Northern clime;
the constant procession of flowers the year through;

the purple hills stretching into the sea; the hundreds
of hamlets, with picturesque homes overgrown with
roses and geranium and heliotrope, in the midst of
orange orchards and of palms and magnolias, in sight
of the snow-peaks of the giant mountain ranges
which shut in this land of marvellous beauty.

CHAPTER IV.

CALIFORNIA is the land of the Pine and the Palm. The tree of the Sierras, native, vigorous, gigantic, and the tree of the Desert, exotic, supple, poetic, both flourish within the nine degrees of latitude. These two, the widely separated lovers of Heine's song, symbolize the capacities of the State, and although the sugar-pine is indigenous, and the date-palm, which will never be more than an ornament in this hospitable soil, was planted by the Franciscan Fathers, who established a chain of missions from San Diego to Monterey over a century ago, they should both be the distinction of one commonwealth, which, in its seven hundred miles of indented sea-coast, can boast the climates of all countries and the products of all zones.

If this State of mountains and valleys were divided by an east and west line, following the general course of the Sierra Madre range, and cutting off the eight lower counties, I suppose there would be conceit enough in either section to maintain that it only is the Paradise of the earth, but both are necessary to make the unique and contradictory California which fascinates and bewilders the traveller. He is told that the inhabitants of San Francisco go away from the draught of the Golden Gate in the summer to get warm, and yet the earliest luscious cherries and apricots which he finds in the far south market of San Diego come from the Northern Santa Clara Valley. The truth would seem to be that in an hour's ride in any part of the State one can change his climate totally at any time of the year, and this not merely by changing his elevation, but by getting in or out of the range of the sea or the desert currents of air which follow the valleys.

To recommend to any one a winter climate is far from the writer's thought. No two persons agree on what is desirable for a winter residence, and the inclination of the same person varies with his state of health. I can only attempt to give some idea of what is called the winter months in Southern California, to which my observations mainly apply. The individual who comes here under the mistaken notion that climate ever does anything more than give nature a better chance, may speedily or more tardily need the service of an undertaker; and the invalid whose powers are responsive to kindly influences may live so long, being unable to get away, that life will be a burden to him. The person in ordinary health will find very little that is hostile to the orderly organic processes. In order to appreciate the winter climate of Southern California one should stay here the year through, and select the days that suit his idea of winter from any of the months. From the fact that the greatest humidity is in the summer and the least in the winter months, he may wear an overcoat in July in a temperature, according to the thermometer, which in January would render the overcoat unnecessary. It is dampness that causes both cold and heat to be most felt. The lowest temperatures, in Southern California generally, are caused only by the extreme dryness of the air; in the long nights of December and January there is a more rapid and longer continued radiation of heat. It must be a dry and clear night that will send the temperature down to thirty-four degrees. But the effect of the sun upon this air is instantaneous, and the cold morning is followed at once by a warm forenoon; the difference between the average heat of July and the average cold of January, measured by the thermometer, is not great in the valleys, foot-hills, and on the coast. Five points give this result of average for January and July respectively: Santa Barbara, 52°, 66°; San Bernardino, 51°, 70°; Pomona, 52°, 68°; Los Angeles, 52°, 67°; San Diego, 53°, 66°. The day in the winter months is warmer in the interior and the nights are cooler than on the coast, as shown by the following figures for January: 7 A.M., Los Angeles, 46.5°; San Diego, 47.5°; 3 P.M., Los Angeles, 65.2°; San Diego, 60.9°. In the summer the difference is greater. In June I saw the thermometer reach 103° in Los Angeles when it was only 79° in San Diego. But I have seen the weather unendurable in New York with a temperature of 85°, while this dry heat of 103° was not oppressive. The extraordinary equanimity of the coast climate (certainly the driest marine climate in my experience) will be evident from the average mean for each month, from records of sixteen years, ending in 1877, taken at San Diego, giving each month in order, beginning with January: 53.5°, 54.7°, 56.0°, 58.2°, 60.2°, 64.6°, 67.1°, 69.0°, 66.7°, 62.9°, 58.1°, 56.0°. In the year 1877 the mean temperature at 3 P.M. at San Diego was as follows, beginning with January: 60.9 , 57.7 , 62.4 , 63.3 , 66.3 , 68.5 , 69.6 , 69.6 , 69.5 , 69.6 , 64.4 , 60.5 . For the four months of July, August, September, and October there was hardly a shade of difference at 3 P.M. The striking fact in all the records I have seen is that the difference of temperature in the daytime between summer and winter is very small, the great difference being from midnight to just before sunrise, and this latter difference is greater inland than on the coast. There are, of course, frost and ice in the mountains, but the frost that comes occasionally in the low inland valleys is of very brief duration in the morning hour, and rarely continues long enough to have a serious effect upon vegetation.

In considering the matter of temperature, the rule for vegetation and for invalids will not be the same. A spot in which delicate flowers in Southern California bloom the year round may be too cool for many invalids. It must not be forgotten that the general temperature here is lower than that to which most Eastern people are accustomed. They are used to living all winter in overheated houses, and to protracted heated terms rendered worse by humidity in the summer. The dry, low temperature of the California winter, notwithstanding its perpetual sunshine, may seem, therefore, wanting to them in direct warmth. It may take a year or two to acclimate them to this more equable and more refreshing temperature.

Neither on the coast nor in the foot-hills will the invalid find the climate of the Riviera or of Tangier —not the tramontane wind of the former, nor the absolutely genial but somewhat enervating climate of the latter. But it must be borne in mind that in this, our Mediterranean, the seeker for health or pleasure can find almost any climate (except the very cold or the very hot), down to the minutest subdivision. He may try the dry marine climate of the coast, or the temperature of the fruit lands and gardens from San Bernardino to Los Angeles, or he may climb to any altitude that suits him in the Sierra Madre or the San Jacinto ranges. The difference may be all-important to him between a valley and a mesa which is not a hundred feet higher; nay, between a valley and the slope of a foot-hill, with a shifting of not more than fifty feet elevation, the change may be as marked for him as it is for the most sensitive young fruit-tree. It is undeniable, notwithstanding these encouraging "averages," that cold snaps, though rare, do come occasionally, just as in summer there will occur one or two or three continued days of intense heat. And in the summer in some localities—it happened in June, 1890, in the Santiago hills in Orange County—the desert sirocco, blowing over the Colorado furnace, makes life just about unendurable for days at a time. Yet with this dry heat sunstroke is never experienced, and the diseases of the bowels usually accompanying hot weather elsewhere are unknown. The experienced traveller who encounters unpleasant weather, heat that he does not expect, cold that he did not provide for, or dust that deprives him of his last atom of good-humor, and is told that it is "exceptional," knows exactly what that word means. He is familiar with the "exceptional" the world over, and he feels a sort of compassion for the inhabitants who have not yet

learned the adage, "Good wine needs no bush."
Even those who have bought more land than they
can pay for can afford to tell the truth.

The rainy season in Southern California, which
may open with a shower or two in October, but does
not set in till late in November, or till December, and
is over in April, is not at all a period of cloudy
weather or continuous rainfall. On the contrary,
bright warm days and brilliant sunshine are the rule.
The rain is most likely to fall in the night. There
may be a day of rain, or several days that are over-
cast with distributed rain, but the showers are soon
over, and the sky clears. Yet winters vary greatly
in this respect, the rainfall being much greater in
some than in others. In 1890 there was rain beyond
the average, and even on the equable beach of Coronado there were some weeks of weather that from
the California point of view were very unpleasant.
It was unpleasant by local comparison, but it was
not damp and chilly, like a protracted period of falling weather on the Atlantic. The rain comes with a
southerly wind, caused by a disturbance far north, and
with the resumption of the prevailing westerly winds
it suddenly ceases, the air clears, and neither before
nor after it is the atmosphere "steamy" or enervating.
The average annual rainfall of the Pacific coast diminishes by regular gradation from point to point all the
way from Puget Sound to the Mexican boundary. At
Neah Bay it is 111 inches, and it steadily lessens down
to Santa Cruz, 25.24; Monterey, 11.42; Point Conception, 12.21; San Diego, 11.01. There is fog on the
coast in every month, but this diminishes, like the
rainfall, from north to south. I have encountered it

in both February and June. In the south it is apt to
be most persistent in April and May, when for three
or four days together there will be a fine mist, which
any one but a Scotchman would call rain. Usually,
however, the fog-bank will roll in during the night,
and disappear by ten o'clock in the morning. There
is no wet season properly so called, and consequently
few days in the winter months when it is not agreeable to be out-of-doors, perhaps no day when one may
not walk or drive during some part of it. Yet as to pre-
cipitation or temperature it is impossible to strike any
general average for Southern California. In 1883-84
San Diego had 25.77 inches of rain, and Los Angeles
(fifteen miles inland) had 38.22. The annual average
at Los Angeles is 17.64; but in 1876-77 the total at
San Diego was only 3.75, and at Los Angeles only
5.28. Yet elevation and distance from the coast do
not always determine the rainfall. The yearly mean
rainfall at Julian, in the San Jacinto range, at an elevation of 4500 feet, is 37.74; observations at Riverside,
1050 feet above the sea, give an average of 9.37.

It is probably impossible to give an Eastern man
a just idea of the winter of Southern California. Accustomed to extremes, he may expect too much. He
wants a violent change. If he quits the snow, the
slush, the leaden skies, the alternate sleet and cold
rain of New England, he would like the tropical heat,
the languor, the color of Martinique. He will not find
them here. He comes instead into a strictly temperate region; and even when he arrives, his eyes deceive him. He sees the orange ripening in its dark
foliage, the long lines of the eucalyptus, the feathery
pepper-tree, the magnolia, the English walnut, the

black live-oak, the fan-palm, in all the vigor of June; everywhere beds of flowers of every hue and of every country blazing in the bright sunlight—the heliotrope, the geranium, the rare hot-house roses overrunning the hedges of cypress, and the scarlet passion-vine climbing to the roof-tree of the cottages; in the vineyard or the orchard the horticulturist is following the cultivator in his shirt-sleeves; he hears running water, the song of birds, the scent of flowers is in the air, and he cannot understand why he needs winter clothing, why he is always seeking the sun, why he wants a fire at night. It is a fraud, he says, all this visible display of summer, and of an almost tropical summer at that; it is really a cold country. It is incongruous that he should be looking at a date-palm in his overcoat, and he is puzzled that a thermometrical heat that should enervate him elsewhere, stimulates him here. The green, brilliant, vigorous vegetation, the perpetual sunshine, deceive him; he is careless about the difference of shade and sun, he gets into a draught, and takes cold. Accustomed to extremes of temperature and artificial heat, I think for most people the first winter here is a disappointment. I was told by a physician who had eighteen years' experience of the climate that in his first winter he thought he had never seen a people so insensitive to cold as the San Diegans, who seemed not to require warmth. And all this time the trees are growing like asparagus, the most delicate flowers are in perpetual bloom, the annual crops are most lusty. I fancy that the soil is always warm. The temperature is truly moderate. The records for a number of years show that the mid-day temperature of clear days in winter is from 60° to 70° on the coast,

4

from 65 to 80 in the interior, while that of rainy days
is about 60 by the sea and inland. Mr. Van Dyke
says that the lowest mid-day temperature recorded at
the United States signal station at San Diego during
eight years is 51. This occurred but once. In those
eight years there were but twenty-one days when the
mid-day temperature was not above 55. In all that
time there were but six days when the mercury fell
below 36 at any time in the night; and but two when
it fell to 32, the lowest point ever reached there. On
one of these two last-named days it went to 51 at
noon, and on the other to 56. This was the great
"cold snap" of December, 1879.

It goes without saying that this sort of climate
would suit any one in ordinary health, inviting and
stimulating to constant out-of-door exercise, and that
it would be equally favorable to that general break-
down of the system which has the name of nervous
prostration. The effect upon diseases of the respiratory organs can only be determined by individual experience. The government has lately been sending
soldiers who have consumption from various stations
in the United States to San Diego for treatment.
This experiment will furnish interesting data. Within a period covering a little over two years, Dr. Hun-
tington, the post surgeon, has had fifteen cases sent
to him. Three of these patients had tubercular consumption; twelve had consumption induced by attacks of pneumonia. One of the tubercular patients
died within a month after his arrival; the second lived
eight months; the third was discharged cured, left the
army, and contracted malaria elsewhere, of which he
died. The remaining twelve were discharged practi-

cally cured of consumption, but two of them subsequently died. It is exceedingly common to meet persons of all ages and both sexes in Southern California who came invalided by disease of the lungs or throat, who have every promise of fair health here, but who dare not leave this climate. The testimony is convincing of the good effect of the climate upon all children, upon women generally, and of its rejuvenating effect upon men and women of advanced years.

CHAPTER V

HEALTH AND LONGEVITY.

IN regard to the effect of climate upon health and longevity, Dr. Remondino quotes old Hufeland that "uniformity in the state of the atmosphere, particularly in regard to heat, cold, gravity, and lightness, contributes in a very considerable degree to the duration of life. Countries, therefore, where great and sudden varieties in the barometer and the thermometer are usual cannot be favorable to longevity. Such countries may be healthy, and many men may become old in them, but they will not attain to a great age, for all rapid variations are so many internal mutations, and these occasion an astonishing consumption both of the forces and the organs." Hufeland thought a marine climate most favorable to longevity. He describes, and perhaps we may say prophesied, a region he had never known, where the conditions and combinations were most favorable to old age, which is epitomized by Dr. Remondino: " where the latitude gives warmth and the sea or ocean tempering winds, where the soil is warm and dry and the sun is also bright and warm, where uninterrupted bright clear weather and a moderate temperature are the rule, where extremes neither of heat nor cold are to be found, where nothing may interfere with the exercise of the aged, and where the actual results and cases of longevity

will bear testimony as to the efficacy of all its climatic
conditions being favorable to a long and comfortable
existence."

In an unpublished paper Dr. Remondino comments
on the extraordinary endurance of animals and men in
the California climate, and cites many cases of uncommon longevity in natives. In reading the accounts of
early days in California I am struck with the endurance of hardship, exposure, and wounds by the natives
and the adventurers, the rancheros, horsemen, herds-
men, the descendants of soldiers and the Indians, their
insensibility to fatigue, and their agility and strength.
This is ascribed to the climate; and what is true of
man is true of the native horse. His only rival in
strength, endurance, speed, and intelligence is the Ara-
bian. It was long supposed that this was racial, and
that but for the smallness of the size of the native
horse, crossing with it would improve the breed of the
Eastern and Kentucky racers. But there was reluctance to cross the finely proportioned Eastern horse
with his diminutive Western brother. The importa-
tion and breeding of thoroughbreds on this coast has
led to the discovery that the desirable qualities of the
California horse were not racial but climatic. The
Eastern horse has been found to improve in size, com-
pactness of muscle, in strength of limb, in wind, with
a marked increase in power of endurance. The traveller here notices the fine horses and their excellent
condition, and the power and endurance of those that
have considerable age. The records made on Eastern
race-courses by horses from California breeding farms
have already attracted attention. It is also remarked
that the Eastern horse is usually improved greatly by

a sojourn of a season or two on this coast, and the plan of bringing Eastern race-horses here for the winter is already adopted.

Man, it is asserted by our authority, is as much benefited as the horse by a change to this climate. The new-comer may have certain unpleasant sensations in coming here from different altitudes and conditions, but he will soon be conscious of better being, of increased power in all the functions of life, more natural and recuperative sleep, and an accession of vitality and endurance. Dr. Remondino also testifies that it occasionally happens in this rejuvenation that families which have seemed to have reached their limit at the East are increased after residence here.

The early inhabitants of Southern California, according to the statement of Mr. H. H. Bancroft and other reports, were found to be living in Spartan conditions as to temperance and training, and in a highly moral condition, in consequence of which they had uncommon physical endurance and contempt for luxury. This training in abstinence and hardship, with temperance in diet, combined with the climate to produce the astonishing longevity to be found here. Contrary to the customs of most other tribes of Indians, their aged were the care of the community. Dr. W. A. Winder, of San Diego, is quoted as saying that in a visit to El Cajon Valley some thirty years ago he was taken to a house in which the aged persons were cared for. There were half a dozen who had reached an extreme age. Some were unable to move, their bony frame being seemingly anchylosed. They were old, wrinkled, and blear-eyed; their skin was hanging in leathery folds about their withered limbs; some had hair as

A TYPICAL GARDEN, NEAR SANTA ANA.

white as snow, and had seen some seven-score of
years; others, still able to crawl, but so aged as to be
unable to stand, went slowly about on their hands and
knees, their limbs being attenuated and withered. The
organs of special sense had in many nearly lost all activity some generations back. Some had lost the use
of their limbs for more than a decade or a generation;
but the organs of life and the "great sympathetic"
still kept up their automatic functions, not recognizing
the fact, and surprisingly indifferent to it, that the rest
of the body had ceased to be of any use a generation
or more in the past. And it is remarked that "these
thoracic and abdominal organs and their physiological
action being kept alive and active, as it were, against
time, and the silent and unconscious functional activity of the great sympathetic and its ganglia, show a
tenacity of the animal tissues to hold on to life that is
phenomenal."

I have no space to enter upon the nature of the
testimony upon which the age of certain Indians here-
after referred to is based. It is such as to satisfy Dr.
Remondino, Dr. Edward Palmer, long connected with
the Agricultural Department of the Smithsonian In-
stitution, and Father A. D. Ubach, who has religious
charge of the Indians in this region. These Indians
were not migratory; they lived within certain limits,
and were known to each other. The missions established by the Franciscan friars were built with the assistance of the Indians. The friars have handed down
by word of mouth many details in regard to their early
missions; others are found in the mission records,
such as carefully kept records of family events—births,
marriages, and deaths. And there is the testimony of

the Indians regarding each other. Father Ubach has
known a number who were employed at the building
of the mission of San Diego (1769–71), a century before he took charge of this mission. These men had
been engaged in carrying timber from the mountains
or in making brick, and many of them were living
within the last twenty years. There are persons still
living at the Indian village of Capitan Grande whose
ages he estimates at over one hundred and thirty
years. Since the advent of civilization the abstemious
habits and Spartan virtues of these Indians have been
impaired, and their care for the aged has relaxed.

Dr. Palmer has a photograph (which I have seen)
of a squaw whom he estimates to be 126 years old.
When he visited her he saw her put six watermelons
in a blanket, tie it up, and carry it on her back for two
miles. He is familiar with Indian customs and history, and a careful cross-examination convinced him
that her information of old customs was not obtained
by tradition. She was conversant with tribal habits
she had seen practised, such as the cremation of the
dead, which the mission fathers had compelled the
Indians to relinquish. She had seen the Indians pun-
ished by the fathers with floggings for persisting in
the practice of cremation.

At the mission of San Tomas, in Lower California,
is still living an Indian (a photograph of whom Dr.
Remondino shows), bent and wrinkled, whose age is
computed at 140 years. Although blind and naked, he
is still active, and daily goes down the beach and along
the beds of the creeks in search of drift-wood, making
it his daily task to gather and carry to camp a fagot of
wood.

Another instance I give in Dr. Remondino's words: "Philip Crossthwaite, who has lived here since 1843, has an old man on his ranch who mounts his horse and rides about daily, who was a grown man breaking horses for the mission fathers when Don Antonio Ser-

OLD ADOBE HOUSE, POMONA.

rano was an infant. Don Antonio I know quite well, having attended him through a serious illness some sixteen years ago. Although now at the advanced age of ninety-three, he is as erect as a pine, and he rides his horse with his usual vigor and grace. He is thin and spare and very tall, and those who knew him fifty years or more remember him as the most skilful horseman in the neighborhood of San Diego. And yet, as fabulous as it may seem, the man who danced this Don Antonio on his knee when he was an infant is not only still alive, but is active enough to mount his horse and canter about the country. Some years ago I attended an elderly gentleman, since dead, who knew this man as a full-grown man when he and Don Serrano were play-children together. From a conversation with Father Ubach I learned that the man's age is perfectly authenticated to be beyond one hundred and eighteen years."

In the many instances given of extreme old age in this region the habits of these Indians have been those of strict temperance and abstemiousness, and their long life in an equable climate is due to extreme simplicity of diet. In many cases of extreme age the diet has consisted simply of acorns, flour, and water. It is asserted that the climate itself induces temperance in drink and abstemiousness in diet. In his estimate of the climate as a factor of longevity, Dr. Remondino says that it is only necessary to look at the causes of death, and the ages most subject to attack, to understand that the less of these causes that are present the greater are the chances of man to reach great age. "Add to these reflections that you run no gantlet of diseases to undermine or deteriorate the organism; that in this climate childhood finds an escape from those diseases which are the terror of mothers, and against which physicians are helpless, as we have here none of those affections of the first three years of life

FAN PALM. FERNANDO ST. LOS ANGELES.

so prevalent during the summer months in the East
and the rest of the United States.   Then, again, the
chance of gastric or intestinal disease is almost incred-.
ibly small.   This immunity extends through every age
of life.   Hepatic and kindred diseases are unknown;
of lung affections there is no land that can boast of
like exemption.   Be it the equability of the tempera-

ture or the aseptic condition of the atmosphere, the
free sweep of winds or the absence of disease germs,
or what else it may be ascribed to, one thing is certain, that there is no pneumonia, bronchitis, or pleu-
risy lying in wait for either the infant or the aged."

The importance of this subject must excuse the
space I have given to it. It is evident from this testimony that here are climatic conditions novel and
worthy of the most patient scientific investigation.
Their effect upon hereditary tendencies and upon persons coming here with hereditary diseases will be
studied. Three years ago there was in some localities
a visitation of small-pox imported from Mexico. At
that time there were cases of pneumonia. Whether
these were incident to carelessness in vaccination, or
were caused by local unsanitary conditions, I do not
know. It is not to be expected that unsanitary conditions will not produce disease here as elsewhere. It
cannot be too strongly insisted that this is a climate
that the new-comer must get used to, and that he
cannot safely neglect the ordinary precautions. The
difference between shade and sun is strikingly marked,
and he must not be deceived into imprudence by the
prevailing sunshine or the general equability.

CHAPTER VI.

IS RESIDENCE HERE AGREEABLE?

AFTER all these averages and statistics, and not considering now the chances of the speculator, the farmer, the fruit-raiser, or the invalid, is Southern California a particularly agreeable winter residence? The question deserves a candid answer, for it is of the last importance to the people of the United States to know the truth — to know whether they have accessible by rail a region free from winter rigor and vicissitudes, and yet with few of the disadvantages of most winter resorts. One would have more pleasure in answering the question if he were not irritated by the perpetual note of brag and exaggeration in every locality that each is the paradise of the earth, and absolutely free from any physical discomfort. I hope that this note of exaggeration is not the effect of the climate, for if it is, the region will never be socially agreeable.

There are no sudden changes of season here. Spring comes gradually day by day, a perceptible hourly waking to life and color; and this glides into a summer which never ceases, but only becomes tired and fades into the repose of a short autumn, when the sere and brown and red and yellow hills and the purple mountains are waiting for the rain clouds. This is according to the process of nature; but

5

wherever irrigation brings moisture to the fertile soil, the green and bloom are perpetual the year round, only the green is powdered with dust, and the cultivated flowers have their periods of exhaustion.

I should think it well worth while to watch the procession of nature here from late November or December to April. It is a land of delicate and brilliant wild flowers, of blooming shrubs, strange in form and wonderful in color. Before the annual rains the land lies in a sort of swoon in a golden haze; the slopes and plains are bare, the hills yellow with ripe wild-oats or ashy gray with sage, the sea-breeze is weak, the air grows drier, the sun hot, the shade cool. Then one day light clouds stream up from the south-west, and there is a gentle rain. When the sun comes out again its rays are milder, the land is refreshed and brightened, and almost immediately a greenish tinge appears on plain and hill-side. At intervals the rain continues, daily the landscape is greener in infinite variety of shades, which seem to sweep over the hills in waves of color. Upon this carpet of green by February nature begins to weave an embroidery of wild flowers, white, lavender, golden, pink, indigo, scarlet, changing day by day and every day more brilliant, and spreading from patches into great fields until dale and hill and table-land are overspread with a refinement and glory of color that would be the despair of the carpet-weavers of Daghestan.

This, with the scent of orange groves and tea-roses, with cool nights, snow in sight on the high mountains, an occasional day of rain, days of bright sunshine, when an overcoat is needed in driving,

must suffice the sojourner for winter. He will be
humiliated that he is more sensitive to cold than the
heliotrope or the violet, but he must bear it. If he
is looking for malaria, he must go to some other
winter resort. If he wants a "norther" continuing
for days, he must move on. If he is accustomed to
various insect pests, he will miss them here. If there
comes a day warmer than usual, it will not be damp
or soggy. So far as nature is concerned there is very
little to grumble at, and one resource of the traveller
is therefore taken away.

But is it interesting? What is there to do? It
must be confessed that there is a sort of monotony
in the scenery as there is in the climate. There is,
to be sure, great variety in a way between coast and
mountain, as, for instance, between Santa Barbara
and Pasadena, and if the tourist will make a business
of exploring the valleys and uplands and cañons little
visited, he will not complain of monotony; but the
artist and the photographer find the same elements
repeated in little varying combinations. There is undeniable repetition in the succession of flower-gardens, fruit orchards, alleys of palms and peppers,
vineyards, and the cultivation about the villas is repeated in all directions. The Americans have not
the art of making houses or a land picturesque. The
traveller is enthusiastic about the exquisite drives
through these groves of fruit, with the ashy or the
snow-covered hills for background and contrast, and
he exclaims at the pretty cottages, vine and rose clad,
in their semi-tropical setting, but if by chance he
comes upon an old adobe or a Mexican ranch house
in the country, he has emotions of a different sort.

There is little left of the old Spanish occupation, but the remains of it make the romance of the country, and appeal to our sense of fitness and beauty. It is to be hoped that all such historical associations will be preserved, for they give to the traveller that which

SCARLET PASSION-VINE.

our country generally lacks, and which is so largely the attraction of Italy and Spain. Instead of adapting and modifying the houses and homes that the climate suggests, the new American comers have brought here from the East the smartness and prettiness of our modern nondescript architecture. The low house, with recesses and galleries, built round an inner court, or *patio*, which, however small, would fill the whole interior with sunshine and the scent of flowers, is the sort of dwelling that would suit the climate and the habit of life here. But the present occupiers have taken no hints from the natives. In village and country they have done all they can, in spite of the maguey and the cactus and the palm and the umbrella-tree and the live-oak and the riotous flowers and the thousand novel forms of vegetation, to give everything a prosaic look. But why should the tourist find fault with this? The American likes it, and he would not like the picturesqueness of the Spanish or the Latin races.

So far as climate and natural beauty go to make one contented in a winter resort, Southern California has unsurpassed attractions, and both seem to me to fit very well the American temperament; but the associations of art and history are wanting, and the tourist knows how largely his enjoyment of a vacation in Southern Italy or Sicily or Northern Africa depends upon these—upon these and upon the aspects of human nature foreign to his experience.

It goes without saying that this is not Europe, either in its human interest or in a certain refinement of landscape that comes only by long cultivation and the occupancy of ages. One advantage of foreign travel to the restless American is that he carries with him no responsibility for the government or the progress of the country he is in, and that he leaves business behind him; whereas in this new country, which is his own, the development of which is so interesting,

and in which the opportunities of fortune seem so inviting, he is constantly tempted "to take a hand in."
If, however, he is superior to this fever, and is willing
simply to rest, to drift along with the equable days, I
know of no other place where he can be more truly
contented. Year by year the country becomes more
agreeable for the traveller, in the first place, through
the improvement in the hotels, and in the second, by
better roads. In the large villages and cities there are
miles of excellent drives, well sprinkled, through delightful avenues, in a park-like country, where the eye
is enchanted with color and luxurious vegetation, and
captivated by the remarkable beauty of the hills, the
wildness and picturesqueness of which enhance the
charming cultivation of the orchards and gardens.
And no country is more agreeable for riding and driving, for even at mid-day, in the direct sun rays, there
is almost everywhere a refreshing breeze, and one rides
or drives or walks with little sense of fatigue. The
horses are uniformly excellent, either in the carriage or
under the saddle. I am sure they are remarkable
in speed, endurance, and ease of motion. If the vis-
iting season had no other attraction, the horses would
make it distinguished.

A great many people like to spend months in a
comfortable hotel, lounging on the piazzas, playing
lawn-tennis, taking a morning ride or afternoon drive,
making an occasional picnic excursion up some mountain cañon, getting up charades, playing at private the-
atricals, dancing, flirting, floating along with more or
less sentiment and only the weariness that comes
when there are no duties. There are plenty of places
where all these things can be done, and with no sort

of anxiety about the weather from week to week, and
with the added advantage that the women and children can take care of themselves.   But for those who
find such a life monotonous there are other resources.
There is very good fishing in the clear streams in the
foot-hills, hunting in the mountains for large game
still worthy of the steadiest nerves, and good bird-
shooting everywhere.   There are mountains to climb,
cañons to explore, lovely valleys in the recesses of the
hills to be discovered—in short, one disposed to activity and not afraid of roughing it could occupy himself
most agreeably and healthfully in the wild parts of
San Bernardino and San Diego counties ; he may even
still start a grizzly in the Sierra Madre range in Los
Angeles County. Hunting and exploring in the mountains, riding over the mesas, which are green from the
winter rains and gay with a thousand delicate grasses
and flowering plants, is manly occupation to suit the
most robust and adventurous.   Those who saunter in
the trim gardens, or fly from one hotel parlor to the
other, do not see the best of Southern California in
the winter.

CHAPTER VII

BUT the distinction of this coast, and that which will forever make it attractive at the season when the North Atlantic is forbidding, is that the ocean-side is as equable, as delightful, in winter as in summer. Its sea-side places are truly all-the-year-round resorts. In subsequent chapters I shall speak in detail of different places as to climate and development and peculiarities of production. I will now only give a general idea of Southern California as a wintering place. Even as far north as Monterey, in the central part of the State, the famous Hotel del Monte, with its magnificent park of pines and live-oaks, and exquisite flower-gardens underneath the trees, is remarkable for its steadiness of temperature. I could see little difference between the temperature of June and of February. The difference is of course greatest at night. The maximum the year through ranges from about 65° to about 80°, and the minimum from about 35° to about 58°, though there are days when the thermometer goes above 90°, and nights when it falls below 30°.

To those who prefer the immediate ocean air to that air as modified by such valleys as the San Gabriel and the Santa Ana, the coast offers a variety of choice in different combinations of sea and mountain

ROSE-BUSH, SANTA BARBARA.

climate all along the southern sunny exposure from
Santa Barbarba to San Diego. In Santa Barbara
County the Santa Inez range of mountains runs westward to meet the Pacific at Point Conception. South
of this noble range are a number of little valleys opening to the sea, and in one of these, with a harbor and
sloping upland and cañon of its own, lies Santa Barbara, looking southward towards the sunny islands of
Santa Rosa and Santa Cruz. Above it is the Mission
Cañon, at the entrance of which is the best-preserved
of the old Franciscan missions. There is a superb
drive eastward along the long and curving sea-beach
of four miles to the cañon of Monticito, which is
rather a series of nooks and terraces, of lovely places
and gardens, of plantations of oranges and figs, rising
up to the base of the gray mountains. The long line
of the Santa Inez suggests the promontory of Sorrento, and a view from the opposite rocky point,
which encloses the harbor on the west, by the help of
cypresses which look like stone-pines, recalls many an
Italian coast scene, and in situation the Bay of Naples.
The whole aspect is foreign, enchanting, and the semi-
tropical fruits and vines and flowers, with a golden
atmosphere poured over all, irresistibly take the mind
to scenes of Italian romance. There is still a little
Spanish flavor left in the town, in a few old houses,
in names and families historic, and in the life without
hurry or apprehension. There is a delightful com-
mingling here of sea and mountain air, and in a hundred fertile nooks in the hills one in the most delicate health may be sheltered from every harsh wind.
I think no one ever leaves Santa Barbara without a
desire to return to it.

Farther down the coast, only eighteen miles from Los Angeles, and a sort of Coney Island resort of that thriving city, is Santa Monica. Its hotel stands on a high bluff in a lovely bend of the coast. It is popular in summer as well as winter, as the number of cottages attest, and it was chosen by the directors of the National Soldiers' Home as the site of the Home on the Pacific coast. There the veterans, in a commodious building, dream away their lives most contentedly, and can fancy that they hear the distant thunder of guns in the pounding of the surf.

At about the same distance from Los Angeles, southward, above Point Vincent, is Redondo Beach, a new resort, which, from its natural beauty and extensive improvements, promises to be a delightful place of sojourn at any time of the year. The mountainous, embracing arms of the bay are exquisite in contour and color, and the beach is very fine. The hotel is perfectly comfortable—indeed, uncommonly attractive—and the extensive planting of trees, palms, and shrubs, and the cultivation of flowers, will change the place in a year or two into a scene of green and floral loveliness; in this region two years, such is the rapid growth, suffices to transform a desert into a park or garden. On the hills, at a little distance from the beach and pier, are the buildings of the Chautauqua, which holds a local summer session here. The Chautauqua people, the country over, seem to have, in selecting sightly and agreeable sites for their temples of education and amusement, as good judgment as the old monks had in planting their monasteries and missions.

If one desires a thoroughly insular climate, he may

cross to the picturesque island of Santa Catalina. All
along the coast flowers bloom in the winter months,
and the ornamental semi-tropical plants thrive; and
there are many striking headlands and pretty bays
and gentle seaward slopes which are already occupied
by villages, and attract visitors who would practise
economy. The hills frequently come close to the
shore, forming those valleys in which the Californians
of the pastoral period placed their ranch houses. At
San Juan Capristrano the fathers had one of their
most flourishing missions, the ruins of which are the
most picturesque the traveller will find. It is altogether a genial, attractive coast, and if the tourist
does not prefer an inland situation, like the Hotel
Raymond (which scarcely has a rival anywhere in its
lovely surroundings), he will keep on down the coast
to San Diego.

The transition from the well-planted counties of
Los Angeles and Orange is not altogether agreeable
to the eye. One misses the trees. The general aspect
of the coast about San Diego is bare in comparison.
This simply means that the southern county is behind
the others in development. Nestled among the hills
there are live-oaks and sycamores; and of course at
National City and below, in El Cajon and the valley
of the Sweetwater, there are extensive plantations of
oranges, lemons, olives, and vines, but the San Diego
region generally lies in the sun shadeless. I have a
personal theory that much vegetation is inconsistent
with the best atmosphere for the human being. The
air is nowhere else so agreeable to me as it is in a
barren New Mexican or Arizona desert at the proper
elevation. I do not know whether the San Diego cli-

mate would be injured if the hills were covered with
forest and the valleys were all in the highest and
most luxuriant vegetation. The theory is that the
interaction of the desert and ocean winds will always keep it as it is, whatever man may do. I can
only say that, as it is, I doubt if it has its equal the
year round for agreeableness and healthfulness in our
Union; and it is the testimony of those whose experience of the best Mediterranean climate is more
extended and much longer continued than mine, that
it is superior to any on that enclosed sea. About this
great harbor, whose outer beach has an extent of
twenty-five miles, whose inland circuit of mountains
must be over fifty miles, there are great varieties of
temperature, of shelter and exposure, minute subdi-
visions of climate, whose personal fitness can only be
attested by experience. There is a great difference,
for instance, between the quality of the climate at the
elevation of the Florence Hotel, San Diego, and the
University Heights on the mesa above the town, and
that on the long Coronado Beach which protects the
inner harbor from the ocean surf. The latter, practically surrounded by water, has a true marine climate,
but a peculiar and dry marine climate, as tonic in its
effect as that of Capri, and, I believe, with fewer harsh
days in the winter season. I wish to speak with entire frankness about this situation, for I am sure that
what so much pleases me will suit a great number
of people, who will thank me for not being reserved.
Doubtless it will not suit hundreds of people as well
as some other localities in Southern California, but I
found no other place where I had the feeling of abso-
lute content and willingness to stay on indefinitely.

There is a geniality about it for which the thermometer does not account, a charm which it is difficult to explain. Much of the agreeability is due to artificial conditions, but the climate man has not made nor marred.

The Coronado Beach is about twelve miles long. A narrow sand promontory, running northward from the main-land, rises to the Heights, then broadens into a table-land, which seems to be an island, and measures about a mile and a half each way; this is called South Beach, and is connected by another spit of sand with a like area called North Beach, which forms, with Point Loma, the entrance to the harbor. The North Beach, covered partly with chaparral and broad fields of barley, is alive with quail, and is a favorite coursing-ground for rabbits. The soil, which appears uninviting, is with water uncommonly fertile, being a mixture of loam, disintegrated granite, and decomposed shells, and especially adapted to flowers, rare tropical trees, fruits, and flowering shrubs of all countries.

The development is on the South Beach, which was in January, 1887, nothing but a waste of sand and chaparral. I doubt if the world can show a like transformation in so short a time. I saw it in February of that year, when all the beauty, except that of ocean, sky, and atmosphere, was still to be imagined. It is now as if the wand of the magician had touched it. In the first place, abundance of water was brought over by a submarine conduit, and later from the extraordinary Coronado Springs (excellent soft water for drinking and bathing, and with a recognized medicinal value), and with these streams the beach began to bloom like a tropical garden. Tens of thousands of trees

6

have attained a remarkable growth in three years.
The nursery is one of the most interesting botanical
and flower gardens in the country: palms and hedges
of Monterey cypress and marguerites line the avenues.
There are parks and gardens of rarest flowers and
shrubs, whose brilliant color produces the same excitement in the mind as strains of martial music. A railway traverses the beach for a mile from the ferry to
the hotel. There are hundreds of cottages with their
gardens scattered over the surface; there is a race-
track, a museum, an ostrich farm, a labyrinth, good
roads for driving, and a dozen other attractions for
the idle or the inquisitive.

The hotel stands upon the south front of the beach
and near the sea, above which it is sufficiently elevated
to give a fine prospect. The sound of the beating surf
is perpetual there. At low tide there is a splendid
driving beach miles in extent, and though the slope
is abrupt, the opportunity for bathing is good, with a
little care in regard to the undertow. But there is a
safe natatorium on the harbor side close to the hotel.
The stranger, when he first comes upon this novel
hotel and this marvellous scene of natural and created
beauty, is apt to exhaust his superlatives. I hesitate
to attempt to describe this hotel—this airy and picturesque and half-bizarre wooden creation of the architect. Taking it and its situation together, I know
nothing else in the world with which to compare it,
and I have never seen any other which so surprised at
first, that so improved on a two weeks' acquaintance,
and that has left in the mind an impression so entirely
agreeable. It covers about four and a half acres of
ground, including an inner court of about an acre, the

HOTEL DEL CORONADO.

rich made soil of which is raised to the level of the
main floor. The house surrounds this, in the Spanish
mode of building, with a series of galleries, so that
most of the suites of rooms have a double outlook—
one upon this lovely garden, the other upon the ocean
or the harbor. The effect of this interior court or
patio is to give gayety and an air of friendliness to
the place, brilliant as it is with flowers and climbing
vines; and when the royal and date palms that are
vigorously thriving in it attain their growth it will be
magnificent. Big hotels and caravansaries are usually
tiresome, unfriendly places; and if I should lay too
much stress upon the vast dining-room (which has a
floor area of ten thousand feet without post or pillar),
or the beautiful breakfast-room, or the circular ball-
room (which has an area of eleven thousand feet, with
its timber roof open to the lofty observatory), or the
music-room, billiard-rooms for ladies, the reading-
rooms and parlors, the pretty gallery overlooking the
spacious office rotunda, and then say that the whole
is illuminated with electric lights, and capable of being heated to any temperature desired—I might convey a false impression as to the actual comfort and
home-likeness of this charming place. On the sea side
the broad galleries of each story are shut in by glass,
which can be opened to admit or shut to exclude the
fresh ocean breeze. Whatever the temperature outside, those great galleries are always agreeable for
lounging or promenading. For me, I never tire of
the sea and its changing color and movement. If this
great house were filled with guests, so spacious are its
lounging places I should think it would never appear
to be crowded; and if it were nearly empty, so ad-

mirably are the rooms contrived for family life it will
not seem lonesome.   I shall add that the management
is of the sort that makes the guest feel at home and at
ease.   Flowers, brought in from the gardens and nurseries, are everywhere in profusion — on the dining-
tables, in the rooms, all about the house.   So abun-

OSTRICH YARD, CORONADO BEACH.

dantly are they produced that no amount of culling
seems to make an impression upon their mass.

But any description would fail to give the secret of
the charm of existence here.   Restlessness disappears,
for one thing, but there is no languor or depression.   I
cannot tell why, when the thermometer is at 60° or
63°, the air seems genial and has no sense of chilliness,

or why it is not oppressive at 80° or 85°. I am sure
the place will not suit those whose highest idea of
winter enjoyment is tobogganing and an ice palace,
nor those who revel in the steam and languor of a
tropical island; but for a person whose desires are
moderate, whose tastes are temperate, who is willing
for once to be good-humored and content in equable
conditions, I should commend Coronado Beach and
the Hotel del Coronado, if I had not long ago learned
that it is unsafe to commend to any human being a
climate or a doctor.

But you can take your choice. It lies there, our
Mediterranean region, on a blue ocean, protected by
barriers of granite from the Northern influences, an
infinite variety of plain, cañon, hills, valleys, sea-coast ;
our New Italy without malaria, and with every sort of
fruit which we desire (except the tropical), which will
be grown in perfection when our knowledge equals our
ambition ; and if you cannot find a winter home there
or pass some contented weeks in the months of Northern inclemency, you are weighing social advantages
against those of the least objectionable climate within
the Union. It is not yet proved that this equability
and the daily out-door life possible there will change
character, but they are likely to improve the disposi-
tion and soften the asperities of common life. At any
rate, there is a land where from November to April
one has not to make a continual fight with the elements to keep alive.

It has been said that this land of the sun and of
the equable climate will have the effect that other
lands of a southern aspect have upon temperament
and habits. It is feared that Northern-bred people,

who are guided by the necessity of making hay while
the sun shines, will not make hay at all in a land
where the sun always shines. It is thought that unless people are spurred on incessantly by the exigen-
cies of the changing seasons they will lose energy, and
fall into an idle floating along with gracious nature.
Will not one sink into a comfortable and easy pro-
crastination if he has a whole year in which to per-
form the labor of three months? Will Southern California be an exception to those lands of equable climate
and extraordinary fertility where every effort is postponed till "to-morrow?"

I wish there might be something solid in this expectation; that this may be a region where the restless American will lose something of his hurry and
petty, feverish ambition. Partially it may be so. He
will take, he is already taking, something of the tone
of the climate and of the old Spanish occupation. But
the race instinct of thrift and of "getting on" will not
wear out in many generations. Besides, the condition
of living at all in Southern California in comfort, and
with the social life indispensable to our people, demands labor, not exhausting and killing, but still incessant — demands industry. A land that will not
yield satisfactorily without irrigation, and whose best
paying produce requires intelligent as well as careful
husbandry, will never be an idle land. Egypt, with
all its *dolce far niente*, was never an idle land for the
laborer.

It may be expected, however, that no more energy
will be developed or encouraged than is needed for the
daily tasks, and these tasks being lighter than elsewhere, and capable of being postponed, that there will

be less stress and strain in the daily life. Although
the climate of Southern California is not enervating,
in fact is stimulating to the new-comer, it is doubtless
true that the monotony of good weather, of the sight
of perpetual bloom and color in orchards and gardens,
will take away nervousness and produce a certain placidity, which might be taken for laziness by a Northern observer. It may be that engagements will not be
kept with desired punctuality, under the impression
that the enjoyment of life does not depend upon exact
response to the second-hand of a watch; and it is not
unpleasant to think that there is a corner of the Union
where there will be a little more leisure, a little more
of serene waiting on Providence, an abatement of the
restless rush and haste of our usual life. The waves
of population have been rolling westward for a long
time, and now, breaking over the mountains, they flow
over Pacific slopes and along the warm and inviting
seas. Is it altogether an unpleasing thought that the
conditions of life will be somewhat easier there, that
there will be some physical repose, the race having
reached the sunset of the continent, comparable to the
desirable placidity of life called the sunset of old age?
This may be altogether fanciful, but I have sometimes
felt, in the sunny moderation of nature there, that this
land might offer for thousands at least a winter of
content.

CHAPTER VIII.

FROM the northern limit of California to the southern is about the same distance as from Portsmouth, New Hampshire, to Charleston, South Carolina. Of these two coast lines, covering nearly ten degrees of latitude, or over seven hundred miles, the Atlantic has greater extremes of climate and greater monthly variations, and the Pacific greater variety of productions. The State of California is, however, so mountainous, cut by longitudinal and transverse ranges, that any reasonable person can find in it a temperature to suit him the year through. But it does not need to be explained that it would be difficult to hit upon any general characteristic that would apply to the stretch of the Atlantic coast named, as a guide to a settler looking for a home; the description of Massachusetts would be wholly misleading for South Carolina. It is almost as difficult to make any comprehensive statement about the long line of the California coast.

It is possible, however, limiting the inquiry to the southern third of the State—an area of about fifty-eight thousand square miles, as large as Maine, New Hampshire, Massachusetts, Connecticut, and Rhode Island—to answer fairly some of the questions oftenest asked about it. These relate to the price of land, its productiveness, the kind of products most profit-

able, the sort of labor required, and its desirability as
a place of residence for the laborer, for the farmer or
horticulturist of small means, and for the man with
considerable capital. Questions on these subjects cannot be answered categorically, but I hope to be able,
by setting down my own observations and using trustworthy reports, to give others the material on which to
exercise their judgment. In the first place, I think it
demonstrable that a person would profitably exchange
160 acres of farming land east of the one hundredth
parallel for ten acres, with a water right, in Southern
California.

In making this estimate I do not consider the question of health or merely the agreeability of the climate, but the conditions of labor, the ease with which
one could support a family, and the profits over and
above a fair living. It has been customary in reckon-
ing the value of land there to look merely to the profit
of it beyond its support of a family, forgetting that
agriculture and horticulture the world over, like almost all other kinds of business, usually do little more
than procure a good comfortable living, with inci-
dental education, to those who engage in them. That
the majority of the inhabitants of Southern California
will become rich by the culture of the orange and the
vine is an illusion; but it is not an illusion that
twenty times its present population can live there in
comfort, in what might be called luxury elsewhere, by
the cultivation of the soil, all far removed from poverty and much above the condition of the majority of
the inhabitants of the foreign wine and fruit-produc-
ing countries. This result is assured by the extraordinary productiveness of the land, uninterrupted the

year through, and by the amazing extension of the market in the United States for products that can be nowhere else produced with such certainty and profusion as in California. That State is only just learning how to supply a demand which is daily increasing, but it already begins to command the market in certain fruits. This command of the market in the future will depend upon itself, that is, whether it will send

YUCCA-PALM.

East and North only sound wine, instead of crude, ill-cured juice of the grape, only the best and most carefully canned apricots, nectarines, peaches, and plums, only the raisins and prunes perfectly prepared, only such oranges, lemons, and grapes and pears as the Californians are willing to eat themselves. California has yet much to learn about fruit-raising and fruit-curing, but it already knows that to compete with the rest of the world in our markets it must beat the rest of the world in quality. It will take some time yet to remove the unfavorable opinion of California wines produced in the East by the first products of the vineyards sent here.

DATE PALM.

The difficulty for the settler is that he cannot "take up" ten acres with water in California as he can 160 acres elsewhere. There is left little available Government land. There is plenty of government land not taken up and which may never be occupied, that is, inaccessible mountain and irreclaimable desert. There are also little nooks and fertile spots here and there to be discovered which may be pre-empted, and which will some day have value. But practically all the arable land, or that is likely to become so, is owned now in large tracts, under grants or by wholesale purchase. The circumstances of the case compelled asso-

ciate effort. Such a desert as that now blooming region known as Pasadena, Pomona, Riverside, and so
on, could not be subdued by individual exertion. Consequently land and water companies were organized.
They bought large tracts of unimproved land, built
dams in the mountain cañons, sunk wells, drew water
from the rivers, made reservoirs, laid pipes, carried
ditches and conduits across the country, and then sold
the land with the inseparable water right in small par-
cels. Thus the region became subdivided among small
holders, each independent, but all mutually dependent
as to water, which is the *sine qua non* of existence. It
is only a few years since there was a forlorn and strug-
gling colony a few miles east of Los Angeles known as
the Indiana settlement. It had scant water, no railway communication, and everything to learn about
horticulture. That spot is now the famous Pasadena.

What has been done in the Santa Ana and San
Gabriel valleys will be done elsewhere in the State.
There are places in Kern County, north of the Sierra
Madre, where the land produces grain and alfalfa without irrigation, where farms can be bought at from five
to ten dollars an acre—land that will undoubtedly increase in value with settlement and also by irrigation.
The great county of San Diego is practically undevel-
oped, and contains an immense area, in scattered mesas
and valleys, of land which will produce apples, grain,
and grass without irrigation, and which the settler can
get at moderate prices. Nay, more, any one with a little ready money, who goes to Southern California ex-
pecting to establish himself and willing to work, will
be welcomed and aided, and be pretty certain to find
some place where he can steadily improve his condi-

tion. But the regions about which one hears most, which are already fruit gardens and well sprinkled with rose-clad homes, command prices per acre which seem extravagant. Land, however, like a mine, gets its value from what it will produce; and it is to be noted that while the subsidence of the "boom" knocked the value out of twenty-feet city lots staked out in the wilderness, and out of insanely inflated city property, the land upon which crops are raised has steadily appreciated in value.

So many conditions enter into the price of land that it is impossible to name an average price for the arable land of the southern counties, but I have heard good judges place it at $100 an acre. The lands, with water, are very much alike in their producing power, but some, for climatic reasons, are better adapted to citrus fruits, others to the raisin grape, and others to deciduous fruits. The value is also affected by railway facilities, contiguity to the local commercial centre, and also by the character of the settlement—that is, by its morality, public spirit, and facilities for education. Every town and settlement thinks it has special advantages as to improved irrigation, equability of temperature, adaptation to this or that product, attractions for invalids, tempered ocean breezes, protection from "northers," schools, and varied industries. These things are so much matter of personal choice that each settler will do well to examine widely for himself, and not buy until he is suited.

Some figures, which may be depended on, of actual sales and of annual yields, may be of service. They are of the district east of Pasadena and Pomona, but fairly represent the whole region down to Los Angeles.

The selling price of raisin grape land unimproved, but
with water, at Riverside is $250 to $300 per acre; at
South Riverside, $150 to $200; in the highland district
of San Bernardino, and at Redlands (which is a new
settlement east of the city of San Bernardino), $200 to
$250 per acre. At Banning and at Hesperia, which lie
north of the San Bernardino range, $125 to $150 per
acre are the prices asked. Distance from the commercial centre accounts for the difference in price in
the towns named. The crop varies with the care and
skill of the cultivator, but a fair average from the
vines at two years is two tons per acre; three years,
three tons; four years, five tons; five years, seven tons.
The price varies with the season, and also whether its
sale is upon the vines, or after picking, drying, and
sweating, or the packed product. On the vines $20
per ton is a fair average price. In exceptional cases
vineyards at Riverside have produced four tons per
acre in twenty months from the setting of the cut-
tings, and six-year-old vines have produced thirteen
and a half tons per acre. If the grower has a crop of,
say, 2000 packed boxes of raisins of twenty pounds
each box, it will pay him to pack his own crop and
establish a "brand" for it. In 1889 three adjoining
vineyards in Riverside, producing about the same
average crops, were sold as follows: The first vineyard, at $17 50 per ton on the vines, yielded $150 per
acre; the second, at six cents a pound, in the sweat
boxes, yielded $276 per acre; the third, at $1 80 per
box, packed, yielded $414 per acre.

Land adapted to the deciduous fruits, such as apricots and peaches, is worth as much as raisin land, and
some years pays better. The pear and the apple need

greater elevation, and are of better quality when grown on high ground than in the valleys. I have reason to believe that the mountain regions of San Diego County are specially adapted to the apple.

Good orange land unimproved, but with water, is worth from $300 to $500 an acre. If we add to this price the cost of budded trees, the care of them for four years, and interest at eight per cent. per annum for four years, the cost of a good grove will be about $1000 an acre. It must be understood that the profit of an orange grove depends upon care, skill, and business ability. The kind of orange grown with reference to the demand, the judgment about more or less irrigation as affecting the quality, the cultivation of the soil, and the arrangements for marketing, are all elements in the problem. There are young groves at Riverside, five years old, that are paying ten per cent. net upon from $3000 to $5000 an acre; while there are older groves, which, at the prices for fruit in the spring of 1890—$1 60 per box for seedlings and $3 per box for navels delivered at the packing-houses—paid at the rate of ten per cent. net on $7500 per acre.

In all these estimates water must be reckoned as a prime factor. What, then, is water worth per inch, generally, in all this fruit region from Redlands to Los Angeles? It is worth just the amount it will add to the commercial value of land irrigated by it, and that may be roughly estimated at from $500 to $1000 an inch of continuous flow. Take an illustration. A piece of land at Riverside below the flow of water was worth $300 an acre. Contiguous to it was another piece not irrigated which would not sell for $50 an acre. By bringing water to it, it would quickly sell

7

for $300, thus adding $250 to its value. As the estimate at Riverside is that one inch of water will irrigate five acres of fruit land, five times $250 would be $1250 per inch, at which price water for irrigation has actually been sold at Riverside.

The standard of measurement of water in Southern California is the miner's inch under four inches' pressure, or the amount that will flow through an inch-square opening under a pressure of four inches measured from the surface of the water in the conduit to the centre of the opening through which it flows. This is nine gallons a minute, or, as it is figured, 1728 cubic feet or 12,960 gallons in twenty-four hours, and 1.50 of a cubic foot a second. This flow would cover ten acres about eighteen inches deep in a year; that is, it would give the land the equivalent of eighteen inches of rain, distributed exactly when and where it was needed, none being wasted, and more serviceable than fifty inches of rainfall as it generally comes. This, with the natural rainfall, is sufficient for citrus fruits and for corn and alfalfa, in soil not too sandy, and it is too much for grapes and all deciduous fruits.

CHAPTER IX.

THE ADVANTAGES OF IRRIGATION.

It is necessary to understand this problem of irrigation in order to comprehend Southern California, the exceptional value of its arable land, the certainty and great variety of its products, and the part it is to play in our markets. There are three factors in the expectation of a crop—soil, sunshine, and water. In a region where we can assume the first two to be constant, the only uncertainty is water. Southern California is practically without rain from May to December. Upon this fact rests the immense value of its soil, and the certainty that it can supply the rest of the Union with a great variety of products. This certainty must be purchased by a previous investment of money. Water is everywhere to be had for money, in some localities by surface wells, in others by artesian-wells, in others from such streams as the Los Angeles and the Santa Ana, and from reservoirs secured by dams in the heart of the high mountains. It is possible to compute the cost of any one of the systems of irrigation, to determine whether it will pay by calculating the amount of land it will irrigate. The cost of procuring water varies greatly with the situation, and it is conceivable that money can be lost in such an investment, but I have yet to hear of any irrigation that has not been more or less successful.

Farming and fruit-raising are usually games of hazard. Good crops and poor crops depend upon enough rain and not too much at just the right times. A wheat field which has a good start with moderate rain may later wither in a drought, or be ruined by too much water at the time of maturity. And, avoiding all serious reverses from either dryness or wet, every farmer knows that the quality and quantity of the product would be immensely improved if the growing stalks and roots could have water when and only when they need it. The difference would be between, say, twenty and forty bushels of grain or roots to the acre, and that means the difference between profit and loss. There is probably not a crop of any kind grown in the great West that would not be immensely benefited if it could be irrigated once or twice a year; and probably anywhere that water is attainable the cost of irrigation would be abundantly paid in the yield from year to year. Farming in the West with even a little irrigation would not be the game of hazard that it is. And it may further be assumed that there is not a vegetable patch or a fruit orchard East or West that would not yield better quality and more abundantly with irrigation.

But this is not all. Any farmer who attempts to raise grass and potatoes and strawberries on contiguous fields, subject to the same chance of drought or rainfall, has a vivid sense of his difficulties. The potatoes are spoiled by the water that helps the grass, and the coquettish strawberry will not thrive on the regimen that suits the grosser crops. In California, which by its climate and soil gives a greater variety of products than any other region in the Union, the supply

of water is adjusted to the needs of each crop, even
on contiguous fields. No two products need the same
amount of water, or need it at the same time. The
orange needs more than the grape, the alfalfa more
than the orange, the peach and apricot less than the
orange; the olive, the fig, the almond, the English walnut, demand each a different supply. Depending en-

RAISIN-CURING.

tirely on irrigation six months of the year, the farmer
in Southern California is practically certain of his crop
year after year; and if all his plants and trees are in
a healthful condition, as they will be if he is not too
idle to cultivate as well as irrigate, his yield will be
about double what it would be without systematic irrigation. It is this practical control of the water the
7*

year round, in a climate where sunshine is the rule,
that makes the productiveness of California so large
as to be incomprehensible to Eastern people. Even
the trees are not dormant more than three or four
months in the year.

But irrigation, in order to be successful, must be
intelligently applied. In unskilful hands it may work
more damage than benefit. Mr. Theodore S. Van Dyke,
who may always be quoted with confidence, says that
the ground should never be flooded; that water must
not touch the plant or tree, or come near enough to
make the soil bake around it; and that it should be let
in in small streams for two or three days, and not in
large streams for a few hours. It is of the first importance that the ground shall be stirred as soon as
dry enough, the cultivation to be continued, and water
never to be substituted for the cultivator to prevent
baking. The methods of irrigation in use may be reduced to three. First, the old Mexican way—running
a small ditch from tree to tree, without any basin round
the tree. Second, the basin system, where a large basin is made round the tree, and filled several times.
This should only be used where water is scarce, for it
trains the roots like a brush, instead of sending them
out laterally into the soil. Third, the Riverside method, which is the best in the world, and produces the
largest results with the least water and the least work.
It is the closest imitation of the natural process of
wetting by gentle rain. "A small flume, eight or ten
inches square, of common red-wood is laid along the
upper side of a ten-acre tract. At intervals of one to
three feet, according to the nature of the ground and
the stuff to be irrigated, are bored one-inch holes, with

a small wooden button over them to regulate the flow.
This flume costs a trifle, is left in position, lasts for
years, and is always ready. Into this flume is turned
from the ditch an irrigating head of 20, 25, or 30 inches
of water, generally about 20 inches. This is divided
by the holes and the buttons into streams of from one-
sixth to one-tenth of an inch each, making from 120
to 200 small streams. From five to seven furrows are
made between two rows of trees, two between rows of
grapes, one furrow between rows of corn, potatoes, etc.
It may take from fifteen to twenty hours for one of the
streams to get across the tract. They are allowed to
run from forty-eight to seventy-two hours. The ground
is then thoroughly wet in all directions, and three or
four feet deep. As soon as the ground is dry enough
cultivation is begun, and kept up from six to eight
weeks before water is used again." Only when the
ground is very sandy is the basin system necessary.
Long experiment has taught that this system is by far
the best; and, says Mr. Van Dyke, "Those whose ideas
are taken from the wasteful systems of flooding or
soaking from big ditches have something to learn in
Southern California."

As to the quantity of water needed in the kind of
soil most common in Southern California I will again
quote Mr. Van Dyke: "They will tell you at Riverside
that they use an inch of water to five acres, and some
say an inch to three acres. But this is because they
charge to the land all the waste on the main ditch, and
because they use thirty per cent. of the water in July
and August, when it is the lowest. But this is no test
of the duty of water; the amount actually delivered
on the land should be taken. What they actually use

for ten acres at Riverside, Redlands, etc., is a twenty-inch stream of three days' run five times a year, equal to 300 inches for one day, or one inch steady run for 300 days. As an inch is the equivalent of 365 inches

IRRIGATION BY ARTESIAN-WELL SYSTEM.

for one day, or one inch for 365 days, 300 inches for one day equals an inch to twelve acres. Many use even less than this, running the water only two or two and a half days at a time. Others use more head; but it rarely exceeds 24 inches for three days and five times a year, which would be 72 multiplied by 5, or 360 inches—a little less than a full inch for a year for ten acres."

I have given room to these details because the Riverside experiment, which results in such large returns of excellent fruit, is worthy of the attention of cultivators everywhere. The constant stirring of the soil, to keep it loose as well as to keep down useless growths, is second in importance only to irrigation. Some years ago, when it was ascertained that tracts of land which had been regarded as only fit for herding cattle and sheep would by good ploughing and constant cultivation produce fair crops without any artificial watering, there spread abroad a notion that irrigation could be dispensed with. There are large areas, dry and cracked on the surface, where the soil is moist three and four feet below the surface in the dry season. By keeping the surface broken and well pulverized the moisture rises sufficiently to insure a crop.

IRRIGATION BY PIPE SYSTEM

Many Western farmers have found out this secret of cultivation, and more will learn in time the good sense of not spreading themselves over too large an area; that forty acres planted and cultivated will give a

better return than eighty acres planted and neglected.
Crops of various sorts are raised in Southern California by careful cultivation with little or no irrigation,
but the idea that cultivation alone will bring sufficiently good production is now practically abandoned, and
the almost universal experience is that judicious irrigation always improves the crop in quality and in
quantity, and that irrigation and cultivation are both
essential to profitable farming or fruit-raising.

CHAPTER X

It would seem, then, that capital is necessary for successful agriculture or horticulture in Southern California. But where is it not needed? In New England? In Kansas, where land which was given to actual settlers is covered with mortgages for money absolutely necessary to develop it? But passing this by, what is the chance in Southern California for laborers and for mechanics? Let us understand the situation. In California there is no exception to the rule that continual labor, thrift, and foresight are essential to the getting of a good living or the gaining of a competence. No doubt speculation will spring up again. It is inevitable with the present enormous and yearly increasing yield of fruits, the better intelligence in vine culture, wine-making, and raisin-curing, the growth of marketable oranges, lemons, etc., and the consequent rise in the value of land. Doubtless fortunes will be made by enterprising companies who secure large areas of unimproved land at low prices, bring water on them, and then sell in small lots. But this will come to an end. The tendency is to subdivide the land into small holdings—into farms and gardens of ten and twenty acres. The great ranches are sure to be broken up. With the resulting settlement by industrious people the cities will again experience "booms;" but these are

not peculiar to California. In my mind I see the time
when this region (because it will pay better propor-
tionally to cultivate a small area) will be one of small
farms, of neat cottages, of industrious homes. The
owner is pretty certain to prosper—that is, to get a
good living (which is independence), and lay aside a
little yearly—if the work is done by himself and his
family. And the peculiarity of the situation is that
the farm or garden, whichever it is called, will give
agreeable and most healthful occupation to all the
boys and girls in the family all the days in the year
that can be spared from the school. Aside from the
ploughing, the labor is light. Pruning, grafting, bud-
ding, the picking of the grapes, the gathering of the
fruit from the trees, the sorting, packing, and canning,
are labor for light and deft hands, and labor distributed through the year. The harvest, of one sort and
another, is almost continuous, so that young girls and
boys can have, in well-settled districts, pretty steady
employment—a long season in establishments packing
oranges; at another time, in canning fruits; at another, in packing raisins.

It goes without saying that in the industries now
developed, and in others as important which are in
their infancy (for instance, the culture of the olive
for oil and as an article of food; the growth and curing of figs; the gathering of almonds, English walnuts,
etc.), the labor of the owners of the land and their
families will not suffice. There must be as large a
proportion of day-laborers as there are in other regions where such products are grown. Chinese labor
at certain seasons has been a necessity. Under the
present policy of California this must diminish, and its

place be taken by some other. The pay for this labor has always been good. It is certain to be more and more in demand. Whether the pay will ever approach near to the European standard is a question, but it is a fair presumption that the exceptional profit of the land, owing to its productiveness, will for a long time keep wages up.

During the "boom" period all wages were high, those of skilled mechanics especially, owing to the great amount of building on speculation. The ordinary laborer on a ranch had $30 a month and board and lodging; laborers of a higher grade, $2 to $2 50 a day; skilled masons, $6; carpenters, from $3 50 to $5; plasterers, $4 to $5; house-servants, from $25 to $35 a month. Since the "boom," wages of skilled mechanics have declined at least 25 per cent., and there has been less demand for labor generally, except in connection with fruit raising and harvesting. It would be unwise for laborers to go to California on an uncertainty, but it can be said of that country with more confidence than of any other section that its peculiar industries, now daily increasing, will absorb an increasing amount of day labor, and later on it will remunerate skilled artisan labor.

In deciding whether Southern California would be an agreeable place of residence there are other things to be considered besides the productiveness of the soil, the variety of products, the ease of out-door labor distributed through the year, the certainty of returns for intelligent investment with labor, the equability of summer and winter, and the adaptation to personal health. There are always disadvantages attending the development of a new country and the evolution of a

new society. It is not a small thing, and may be one
of daily discontent, the change from a landscape clad
with verdure, the riotous and irrepressible growth of a
rainy region, to a land that the greater part of the year
is green only where it is artificially watered, where all

GARDEN SCENE, SANTA ANA.

the hills and unwatered plains are brown and sere,
where the foliage is coated with dust, and where driving anywhere outside the sprinkled avenues of a town
is to be enveloped in a cloud of powdered earth. This

discomfort must be weighed against the commercial
advantages of a land of irrigation.

What are the chances for a family of very moderate means to obtain a foothold and thrive by farming
in Southern California? I cannot answer this better
than by giving substantially the experience of one
family, and by saying that this has been paralleled,
with change of details, by many others. Of course, in
a highly developed settlement, where the land is
mostly cultivated, and its actual yearly produce makes
its price very high, it is not easy to get a foothold.
But there are many regions—say in Orange County,
and certainly in San Diego—where land can be had at
a moderate price and on easy terms of payment. Indeed, there are few places, as I have said, where an
industrious family would not find welcome and cordial
help in establishing itself. And it must be remem-
bered that there are many communities where life is
very simple, and the great expense of keeping up an
appearance attending life elsewhere need not be reckoned.

A few years ago a professional man in a New England city, who was in delicate health, with his wife
and five boys, all under sixteen, and one too young to
be of any service, moved to San Diego. He had in
money a small sum, less than a thousand dollars. He
had no experience in farming or horticulture, and his
health would not have permitted him to do much field
work in our climate. Fortunately he found in the fertile El Cajon Valley, fifteen miles from San Diego, a
farmer and fruit-grower, who had upon his place a
small unoccupied house. Into that house he moved,
furnishing it very simply with furniture bought in San

Diego, and hired his services to the landlord. The work required was comparatively easy, in the orchard and vineyards, and consisted largely in superintending other laborers. The pay was about enough to support his family without encroaching on his little capital. Very soon, however, he made an arrangement to buy the small house and tract of some twenty acres on which he lived, on time, perhaps making a partial payment. He began at once to put out an orange orchard and plant a vineyard; this he accomplished with the assistance of his boys, who did practically most of the work after the first planting, leaving him a chance to give most of his days to his employer. The orchard and vineyard work is so light that a smart, intelligent boy is almost as valuable a worker in the field as a man. The wife, meantime, kept the house and did its work. House-keeping was comparatively easy; little fuel was required except for cooking; the question of clothes was a minor one. In that climate wants for a fairly comfortable existence are fewer than with us. From the first, almost, vegetables, raised upon the ground while the vines and oranges were growing, contributed largely to the support of the family. The out-door life and freedom from worry insured better health, and the diet of fruit and vegetables, suitable to the climate, reduced the cost of living to a minimum. As soon as the orchard and the vineyard began to produce fruit, the owner was enabled to quit working for his neighbor, and give all his time to the development of his own place. He increased his planting; he added to his house; he bought a piece of land adjoining which had a grove of eucalyptus, which would supply him with fuel. At first the society cir-

cle was small, and there was no school; but the in-
coming of families had increased the number of children, so that an excellent public school was established.
When I saw him he was living in conditions of comfortable industry; his land had trebled in value; the
pair of horses which he drove he had bought cheap,
for they were Eastern horses; but the climate had
brought them up, so that the team was a serviceable
one in good condition. The story is not one of brilliant success, but to me it is much more hopeful for
the country than the other tales I heard of sudden
wealth or lucky speculation. It is the founding in an
unambitious way of a comfortable home. The boys of
the family will branch out, get fields, orchards, vineyards of their own, and add to the solid producing industry of the country. This orderly, contented industry, increasing its gains day by day, little by little, is
the life and hope of any State.

8

CHAPTER XI.

IT is not the purpose of this volume to describe Southern California. That has been thoroughly done; and details, with figures and pictures in regard to every town and settlement, will be forthcoming on application, which will be helpful guides to persons who can see for themselves, or make sufficient allowance for local enthusiasm. But before speaking further of certain industries south of the great mountain ranges, the region north of the Sierra Madre, which is allied to Southern California by its productions, should be mentioned. The beautiful antelope plains and the Kern Valley (where land is still cheap and very productive) should not be overlooked. The splendid San Joaquin Valley is already speaking loudly and clearly for itself. The region north of the mountains of Kern County, shut in by the Sierra Nevada range on the east and the Coast Range on the west, substantially one valley, fifty to sixty miles in breadth, watered by the King and the San Joaquin, and gently sloping to the north, say for two hundred miles, is a land of marvellous capacity, capable of sustaining a dense population. It is cooler in winter than Southern California, and the summers average much warmer. Owing to the greater heat, the fruits mature sooner. It is just now becoming celebrated for its raisins, which in qual-

ity are unexcelled; and its area, which can be well irrigated from the rivers and from the mountains on
either side, seems capable of producing raisins enough
to supply the world. It is a wonderfully rich valley
in a great variety of products. Fresno County, which
occupies the centre of this valley, has 1,200,000 acres
of agricultural and 4,400,000 of mountain and pasture
land. The city of Fresno, which occupies land that in
1870 was a sheep ranch, is the commercial centre of a
beautiful agricultural and fruit region, and has a population estimated at 12,000. From this centre were
shipped in the season of 1890, 1500 car-loads of raisins.
In 1865 the only exports of Fresno County were a few
bales of wool. The report of 1889 gave a shipment of
700,000 boxes of raisins, and the whole export of 1890,
of all products, was estimated at $10,000,000. Wheth-
er these figures are exact or not, there is no doubt of
the extraordinary success of the raisin industry, nor
that this is a region of great activity and promise.

The traveller has constantly to remind himself that
this is a new country, and to be judged as a new country. It is out of his experience that trees can grow so
fast, and plantations in so short a time put on an appearance of maturity. When he sees a roomy, pretty
cottage overrun with vines and flowering plants, set in
the midst of trees and lawns and gardens of tropical
appearance and luxuriance, he can hardly believe that
three years before this spot was desert land. When
he looks over miles of vineyards, of groves of oranges,
olives, walnuts, prunes, the trees all in vigorous bearing, he cannot believe that five or ten years before the
whole region was a waste. When he enters a handsome village, with substantial buildings of brick, and

perhaps of stone, with fine school-houses, banks, hotels, an opera-house, large packing-houses, and ware-
houses and shops of all sorts, with tasteful dwellings
and lovely ornamented lawns, it is hard to understand

A GRAPE-VINE, MONTECITO VALLEY, SANTA BARBARA.

that all this is the creation of two or three years. Yet
these surprises meet the traveller at every turn, and
the wonder is that there is not visible more crudeness,
eccentric taste, and evidence of hasty beginnings.

San Bernardino is comparatively an old town. It

was settled in 1853 by a colony of Mormons from Salt
Lake. The remains of this colony, less than a hundred, still live here, and have a church like the other
sects, but they call themselves Josephites, and do not
practise polygamy. There is probably not a sect or
schism in the United States that has not its represent-
ative in California. Until 1865 San Bernardino was
merely a straggling settlement, and a point of distribution for Arizona. The discovery that a large part of
the county was adapted to the orange and the vine,
and the advent of the Santa Fé railway, changed all
that. Land that then might have been bought for
$4 an acre is now sold at from $200 to $300, and the
city has become the busy commercial centre of a large
number of growing villages, and of one of the most
remarkable orange and vine districts in the world. It
has many fine buildings, a population of about 6000,
and a decided air of vigorous business. The great
plain about it is mainly devoted to agricultural products, which are grown without irrigation, while in the
near foot-hills the orange and the vine flourish by the
aid of irrigation. Artesian-wells abound in the San
Bernardino plain, but the mountains are the great and
unfailing source of water supply. The Bear Valley
Dam is a most daring and gigantic construction. A
solid wall of masonry, 300 feet long and 60 feet high,
curving towards the reservoir, creates an inland lake in
the mountains holding water enough to irrigate 20,000
acres of land. This is conveyed to distributing reservoirs in the east end of the valley. On a terrace in
the foot-hills a few miles to the north, 2000 feet above
the sea, are the Arrow-head Hot Springs (named from
the figure of a gigantic "arrow-head" on the mount-

ain above), already a favorite resort for health and pleasure. The views from the plain of the picturesque foot-hills and the snow-peaks of the San Bernardino range are exceedingly fine. The marvellous beauty of the purple and deep violet of the giant hills at sunset, with spotless snow, lingers in the memory.

Perhaps the settlement of Redlands, ten miles by rail east of San Bernardino, is as good an illustration as any of rapid development and great promise. It is devoted to the orange and the grape. As late as 1875 much of it was Government land, considered value-less. It had a few settlers, but the town, which counts now about 2000 people, was only begun in 1887. It has many solid brick edifices and many pretty cottages on its gentle slopes and rounded hills, overlooked by the great mountains. The view from any point of vantage of orchards and vineyards and semi-tropical gardens, with the wide sky-line of noble and snow-clad hills, is exceedingly attractive. The region is watered by the Santa Ana River and Mill Creek, but the main irrigating streams, which make every hill-top to bloom with vegetation, come from the Bear Valley Reservoir. On a hill to the south of the town the Smiley Brothers, of Catskill fame, are building fine residences, and plant-ing their 125 acres with fruit-trees and vines, ever-greens, flowers, and semi-tropic shrubbery in a style of landscape-gardening that in three years at the fur-thest will make this spot one of the few great show-places of the country. Behind their ridge is the San Mateo Cañon, through which the Southern Pacific Railway runs, while in front are the splendid sloping plains, valleys, and orange groves, and the great sweep of mountains from San Jacinto round to the Sierra

Madre range. It is almost a matchless prospect. The climate is most agreeable, the plantations increase month by month, and thus far the orange-trees have not been visited by the scale, nor the vines by any sickness. Although the groves are still young, there were shipped from Redlands in the season of 1889–90 80 car-loads of oranges, of 286 boxes to the car, at a price averaging nearly $1000 a car. That season's planting of oranges was over 1200 acres. It had over 5000 acres in fruits, of which nearly 3000 were in peaches, apricots, grapes, and other sorts called deciduous.

Riverside may without prejudice be regarded as the centre of the orange growth and trade. The railway shipments of oranges from Southern California in the season of 1890 aggregated about 2400 car-loads, or about 800,000 boxes, of oranges (in which estimate the lemons are included), valued at about $1,500,000. Of this shipment more than half was from Riverside. This has been, of course, greatly stimulated by the improved railroad facilities, among them the shortening of the time to Chicago by the Santa Fé route, and the running of special fruit trains. Southern California responds like magic to this chance to send her fruits to the East, and the area planted month by month is something enormous. It is estimated that the crop of oranges alone in 1891 will be over 4500 car-loads. We are accustomed to discount all California estimates, but I think that no one yet has comprehended the amount to which the shipments to Eastern markets of vegetables and fresh and canned fruits will reach within five years. I base my prediction upon some observation of the Eastern demand and the re-

ports of fruit-dealers, upon what I saw of the new
planting all over the State in 1890, and upon the statistics of increase. Take Riverside as an example.
In 1872 it was a poor sheep ranch. In 1880–81 it
shipped 15 car-loads, or 4290 boxes, of oranges; the
amount yearly increased, until in 1888–89 it was 925
car-loads, or 263,879 boxes. In 1890 it rose to 1253
car-loads, or 358,341 boxes; and an important fact is
that the largest shipment was in April (455 car-loads,
or 130,226 boxes), at the time when the supply from
other orange regions for the markets East had nearly
ceased.

It should be said, also, that the quality of the
oranges has vastly improved. This is owing to better
cultivation, knowledge of proper irrigation, and the

IRRIGATING AN ORCHARD.

adoption of the best va-
rieties for the soil. As
different sorts of or-
anges mature at differ-
ent seasons, a variety is
needed to give edible
fruit in each month from
December to May inclu-
sive. In February, 1887,
I could not find an or-
ange of the first class
compared with the best
fruit in other regions. It may have been too early
for the varieties I tried; but I believe there has been
a marked improvement in quality. In May, 1890,
we found delicious oranges almost everywhere. The
seedless Washington and Australian navels are fa-
vorites, especially for the market, on account of their

ORANGE CULTURE.

Packing Oranges—Navel Orange-tree Six Years Old—Irrigating an Orange Grove.

great size and fine color. When in perfection they
are very fine, but the skin is thick and the texture
coarser than that of some others. The best orange
I happened to taste was a Tahiti seedling at Montecito (Santa Barbara). It is a small orange, with a
thin skin and a compact, sweet pulp that leaves little fibre. It resembles the famous orange of Malta.
But there are many excellent varieties — the Mediterranean sweet, the paper rind St. Michael, the Maltese
blood, etc. The experiments with seedlings are profitable, and will give ever new varieties. I noted that
the "grape fruit," which is becoming so much liked
in the East, is not appreciated in California.

The city of Riverside occupies an area of some five
miles by three, and claims to have 6000 inhabitants;
the centre is a substantial town with fine school and
other public buildings, but the region is one succession
of orange groves and vineyards, of comfortable houses
and broad avenues. One avenue through which we
drove is 125 feet wide and 12 miles long, planted in
three rows with palms, magnolias, the *Grevillea robusta*
(Australian fern), the pepper, and the eucalyptus, and
lined all the way by splendid orange groves, in the
midst of which are houses and grounds with semi-
tropical attractions. Nothing could be lovelier than
such a scene of fruits and flowers, with the background of purple hills and snowy peaks. The mountain views are superb. Frost is a rare visitor. Not
in fifteen years has there been enough to affect the
orange. There is little rain after March, but there are
fogs and dew-falls, and the ocean breeze is felt daily.
The grape grown for raisins is the muscat, and this
has had no "sickness." Vigilance and a quarantine

have also kept from the orange the scale which has
been so annoying in some other localities. The
orange, when cared for, is a generous bearer; some
trees produce twenty boxes each, and there are areas
of twenty acres in good bearing which have brought
to the owner as much as $10,000 a year.

The whole region of the Santa Ana and San Gabriel valleys, from the desert on the east to Los Angeles, the city of gardens, is a surprise, and year by year
an increasing wonder. In production it exhausts the
catalogue of fruits and flowers; its scenery is varied
by ever new combinations of the picturesque and the
luxuriant; every town boasts some special advantage
in climate, soil, water, or society; but these differences,
many of them visible to the eye, cannot appear in any
written description. The traveller may prefer the
scenery of Pasadena, or that of Pomona, or of Riverside, but the same words in regard to color, fertility,
combinations of orchards, avenues, hills, must appear
in the description of each. Ontario, Pomona, Puente,
Alhambra—wherever one goes there is the same wonder of color and production.

Pomona is a pleasant city in the midst of fine
orange groves, watered abundantly by artesian-wells
and irrigating ditches from a mountain reservoir. A
specimen of the ancient adobe residence is on the
Meserve plantation, a lovely old place, with its gardens
of cherries, strawberries, olives, and oranges. From
the top of San José hill we had a view of a plain
twenty-five miles by fifty in extent, dotted with cultivation, surrounded by mountains—a wonderful prospect. Pomona, like its sister cities in this region, has
a regard for the intellectual side of life, exhibited in

good school-houses and public libraries.   In the libra-
ry of Pomona is what may be regarded as the tutelary
deity of the place—the goddess Pomona, a good copy
in marble of the famous statue in the Ufizi Gallery,
presented to the city by the Rev. C. F. Loop.   This
enterprising citizen is making valuable experiments
in olive culture, raising a dozen varieties in order to
ascertain which is best adapted to this soil, and which
will make the best return in oil and in a marketable
product of cured fruit for the table.

The growth of the olive is to be, it seems to me,
one of the leading and most permanent industries of
Southern California.   It will give us, what it is nearly
impossible to buy now, pure olive oil, in place of the
cotton-seed and lard mixture in general use.   It is a
most wholesome and palatable article of food.   Those
whose chief experience of the olive is the large, coarse,
and not agreeable Spanish variety, used only as an ap-
petizer, know little of the value of the best varieties as
food, nutritious as meat, and always delicious.   Good
bread and a dish of pickled olives make an excellent
meal.   The sort known as the Mission olive, planted
by the Franciscans a century ago, is generally grown
now, and the best fruit is from the older trees.   The
most successful attempts in cultivating the olive and
putting it on the market have been made by Mr. F. A.
Kimball, of National City, and Mr. Ellwood Cooper,
of Santa Barbara.   The experiments have gone far
enough to show that the industry is very remunera-
tive.   The best olive oil I have ever tasted anywhere
is that produced from the Cooper and the Kimball
orchards; but not enough is produced to supply the
local demand.   Mr. Cooper has written a careful trea-

IN A FIELD
OF GOLDEN PUMPKINS.

tise on olive culture, which will be of great service to
all growers. The art of pickling is not yet mastered,
and perhaps some other variety will be preferred to
the old Mission for the table. A mature olive grove
in good bearing is a fortune. I feel sure that within
twenty-five years this will be one of the most profitable industries of California, and that the demand for
pure oil and edible fruit in the United States will drive
out the adulterated and inferior present commercial
products. But California can easily ruin its reputation by adopting the European systems of adultera-
tion.

We drove one day from Arcadia Station through

the region occupied by the Baldwin plantations, an area of over fifty thousand acres—a happy illustration of what industry and capital can do in the way of variety of productions, especially in what are called the San Anita vineyards and orchards, extending southward from the foot-hills. About the home place and in many sections where the irrigating streams flow one might fancy he was in the tropics, so abundant and brilliant are the flowers and exotic plants. There are splendid orchards of oranges, almonds, English walnuts, lemons, peaches, apricots, figs, apples, and olives, with grain and corn—in short, everything that grows in garden or field. The ranch is famous for its brandies and wines as well as fruits. We lunched at the East San Gabriel Hotel, a charming place with a peaceful view from the wide veranda of live-oaks, orchards, vineyards, and the noble Sierra Madre range. The Californians may be excused for using the term paradisiacal about such scenes. Flowers, flowers everywhere, color on color, and the song of the mocking-bird!

CHAPTER XII.

IN the San Gabriel Valley and elsewhere I saw evidence of the perils that attend the culture of the vine and the fruit-tree in all other countries, and from which California in the early days thought it was exempt. Within the past three or four years there has prevailed a sickness of the vine, the cause of which is unknown, and for which no remedy has been discovered. No blight was apparent, but the vine sickened and failed. The disease was called consumption of the vine. I saw many vineyards subject to it, and hundreds of acres of old vines had been rooted up as useless. I was told by a fruit-buyer in Los Angeles that he thought the raisin industry below Fresno was ended unless new planting recovered the vines, and that the great wine fields were about "played out." The truth I believe to be that the disease is confined to the vineyards of Old Mission grapes. Whether these had attained the limit of their active life, and sickened, I do not know. The trouble for a time was alarming; but new plantings of other varieties of grapes have been successful, the vineyards look healthful, and the growers expect no further difficulty. The planting, which was for a time suspended, has been more vigorously renewed.

The insect pests attacking the orange were even more serious, and in 1887–88, though little was published about it, there was something like a panic, in the fear that the orange and lemon culture in Southern California would be a failure. The enemies were the black, the red, and the white scale. The latter, the *icerya purchasi*, or cottony cushion scale, was especially loathsome and destructive; whole orchards were enfeebled, and no way was discovered of staying its progress, which threatened also the olive and every other tree, shrub, and flower. Science was called on to discover its parasite. This was found to be the Australian lady-bug (*vedolia cardinalis*), and in 1888–89 quantities of this insect were imported and spread throughout Los Angeles County, and sent to Santa Barbara and other afflicted districts. The effect was magical. The *vedolia* attacked the cottony scale with intense vigor, and everywhere killed it. The orchards revived as if they had been recreated, and the danger was over. The enemies of the black and the red scale have not yet been discovered, but they probably will be. Meantime the growers have recovered courage, and are fertilizing and fumigating. In Santa Ana I found that the red scale was fought successfully by fumigating the trees. The operation is performed at night under a movable tent, which covers the tree. The cost is about twenty cents a tree. One lesson of all this is that trees must be fed in order to be kept vigorous to resist such attacks, and that fruit-raising, considering the number of enemies that all fruits have in all climates, is not an idle occupation. The clean, handsome English walnut is about the only tree in the State that thus far has no enemy.

9

One cannot take anywhere else a more exhila-
rating, delightful drive than about the rolling, highly
cultivated, many-villaed Pasadena, and out to the foot-
hills and the Sierra Madre Villa. He is constantly ex-
claiming at the varied loveliness of the scene—oranges,
palms, formal gardens, hedges of Monterey cypress. It
is very Italy-like. The Sierra Madre furnishes abundant water for all the valley, and the swift irrigating
stream from Eaton Cañon waters the Sierra Madre
Villa. Among the peaks above it rises Mt. Wilson,
a thousand feet above the plain, the site selected for
the Harvard Observatory with its 40-inch glass. The
clearness of the air at this elevation, and the absence
of clouds night and day the greater portion of the
year, make this a most advantageous position, it is
said, to use the glass in dissolving nebulae. The Sierra
Madre Villa, once the most favorite resort in this region, was closed. In its sheltered situation, its luxuriant and half-neglected gardens, its wide plantations
and irrigating streams, it reminds one of some secu-
larized monastery on the promontory of Sorrento. It
only needs good management to make the hotel very
attractive and especially agreeable in the months of
winter.

Pasadena, which exhibits everywhere evidences of
wealth and culture, and claims a permanent population of 12,000, has the air of a winter resort; the great
Hotel Raymond is closed in May, the boarding-houses
want occupants, the shops and livery-stables custom-
ers, and the streets lack movement. This is easily
explained. It is not because Pasadena is not an agreeable summer residence, but because the visitors are
drawn there in the winter principally to escape the

PACKING CHERRIES, PODOLIA.

inclement climate of the North and East, and because
special efforts have been made for their entertainment
in the winter. We found the atmosphere delightful
in the middle of May. The mean summer heat is 67 ,
and the nights are always cool. The hills near by may
be resorted to with the certainty of finding as decided
a change as one desires in the summer season. I must
repeat that the Southern California summer is not at
all understood in the East. The statement of the general equability of the temperature the year through
must be insisted on. We lunched one day in a typical
California house, in the midst of a garden of fruits,
flowers, and tropical shrubs; in a house that might
be described as half roses and half tent, for added to
the wooden structure were rooms of canvas, which are
used as sleeping apartments winter and summer.

This attractive region, so lovely in its cultivation,
with so many charming drives, offering good shooting
on the plains and in the hills, and centrally placed for
excursions, is only eight miles from the busy city of
Los Angeles. An excellent point of view of the country is from the graded hill on which stands the Raymond Hotel, a hill isolated but easy of access, which
is in itself a mountain of bloom, color, and fragrance.
From all the broad verandas and from every window
the prospect is charming, whether the eye rests upon
cultivated orchards and gardens and pretty villas, or
upon the purple foot-hills and the snowy ranges. It
enjoys a daily ocean breeze, and the air is always ex-
hilarating. This noble hill is a study in landscape-
gardening. It is a mass of brilliant color, and the hos-
pitality of the region generally to foreign growths may
be estimated by the trees acclimated on these slopes.

They are the pepper, eucalyptus, pine, cyprus, syca-
more, red-wood, olive, date and fan palms, banana,
pomegranate, guava, Japanese persimmon, umbrella,
maple, elm, locust, English walnut, birch, ailantus, pop-
lar, willow, and more ornamental shrubs than one can
well name.

I can indulge in few locality details except those
which are illustrative of the general character of the
country. In passing into Orange County, which was
recently set off from Los Angeles, we come into a region of less " fashion," but one that for many reasons
is attractive to people of moderate means who are
content with independent simplicity. The country
about the thriving village of Santa Ana is very rich,
being abundantly watered by the Santa Ana River and
by artesian-wells. The town is nine miles from the
ocean. On the ocean side the land is mainly agricultural; on the inland side it is specially adapted to
fruit. We drove about it, and in Tustin City, which
has many pleasant residences and a vacant " boom "
hotel, through endless plantations of oranges. On the
road towards Los Angeles we passed large herds of
cattle and sheep, and fine groves of the English walnut, which thrives especially well in this soil and the
neighborhood of the sea. There is comparatively little waste land in this valley district, as one may see
by driving through the country about Santa Ana,
Orange, Anaheim, Tustin City, etc. Anaheim is a
prosperous German colony. It was here that Madame
Modjeska and her husband, Count Bozenta, first settled in California. They own and occupy now a picturesque ranch in the Santiago Cañon of the Santa
Ana range, twenty-two miles from Santa Ana. This

is one of the richest regions in the State, and with its fair quota of working population, it will be one of the most productive.

From Newport, on the coast, or from San Pedro, one may visit the island of Santa Catalina. Want of time prevented our going there. Sportsmen enjoy there the exciting pastime of hunting the wild goat. From the photographs I saw, and from all I heard of it, it must be as picturesque a resort in natural beauty as the British Channel islands.

Los Angeles is the metropolitan centre of all this region. A handsome, solid, thriving city, environed by gardens, gay everywhere with flowers, it is too well known to require any description from me. To the traveller from the East it will always be a surprise. Its growth has been phenomenal, and although it may not equal the expectations of the crazy excitement of 1886-87, 50,000 people is a great assemblage for a new city which numbered only about 11,000 in 1880. It of course felt the subsidence of the "boom," but while I missed the feverish crowds of 1887, I was struck with its substantial progress in fine, solid buildings, pavements, sewerage, railways, educational facilities, and ornamental grounds. It has a secure hold on the commerce of the region. The assessment roll of the city increased from $7,627,632 in 1881 to $44,871,073 in 1889. Its bank business, public buildings, school-houses, and street improvements are in accord with this increase, and show solid, vigorous growth. It is altogether an attractive city, whether seen on a drive through its well-planted and bright avenues, or looked down on from the hills which are climbed by the cable roads. A curious social note was the effect of the

"boom" excitement upon the birth rate. The report
of children under the age of one year was in 1887,
271 boy babies and 264 girl babies; from 1887 to 1888
there were only 176 boy babies and 162 girl babies.
The return at the end of 1889 was 465 boy babies, and
500 girl babies.

Although Los Angeles County still produces a considerable quantity of wine and brandy, I have an im-

OLIVE-TREES SIX YEARS OLD.

pression that the raising of raisins will supplant wine-
making largely in Southern California, and that the
principal wine producing will be in the northern portions of the State. It is certain that the best quality is

grown in the foot-hills. The reputation of "California wines" has been much injured by placing upon the market crude juice that was in no sense wine. Great improvement has been made in the past three to five years, not only in the vine and knowledge of the soil adapted to it, but in the handling and the curing of the wine. One can now find without much difficulty excellent table wines—sound claret, good white Reisling, and sauterne. None of these wines are exactly like the foreign wines, and it may be some time before the taste accustomed to foreign wines is educated to like them. But in Eastern markets some of the best brands are already much called for, and I think it only a question of time and a little more experience when the best California wines will be popular. I found in the San Francisco market excellent red wines at $3.50 the case, and what was still more remarkable, at some of the best hotels sound, agreeable claret at from fifteen to twenty cents the pint bottle.

It is quite unnecessary to emphasize the attractions of Santa Barbara, or the productiveness of the valleys in the counties of Santa Barbara and Ventura. There is no more poetic region on the continent than the bay south of Point Conception, and the pen and the camera have made the world tolerably familiar with it. There is a graciousness, a softness, a color in the sea, the cañons, the mountains there that dwell in the memory. It is capable of inspiring the same love that the Greek colonists felt for the region between the bays of Salerno and Naples. It is as fruitful as the Italian shores, and can support as dense a population. The figures that have been given as to productiveness and variety of productions apply to it. Hav-

ing more winter rainfall than the counties south of
it, agriculture is profitable in most years. Since the
railway was made down the valley of the Santa Clara
River and along the coast to Santa Barbara, a great
impulse has been given to farming. Orange and other
fruit orchards have increased. Near Buenaventura I
saw hundreds of acres of lima beans. The yield is
about one ton to the acre. With good farming the
valleys yield crops of corn, barley, and wheat much
above the average. Still it is a fruit region, and no
variety has yet been tried that does not produce very
well there. The rapid growth of all trees has enabled
the region to demonstrate in a short time that there
is scarcely any that it cannot naturalize. The curious growths of tropical lands, the trees of aromatic
and medicinal gums, the trees of exquisite foliage and
wealth of fragrant blossoms, the sturdy forest natives,
and the bearers of edible nuts are all to be found
in the gardens and by the road-side, from New England, from the Southern States, from Europe, from
North and South Africa, Southern Asia, China, Japan,
from Australia and New Zealand and South America.
The region is an arboreal and botanical garden on an
immense scale, and full of surprises. The floriculture
is even more astonishing. Every land is represented.
The profusion and vigor are as wonderful as the variety. At a flower show in Santa Barbara were exhibited 160 varieties of roses all cut from one garden the
same morning. The open garden rivals the Eastern
conservatory. The country is new and many of the
conditions of life may be primitive and rude, but it
is impossible that any region shall not be beautiful,
clothed with such a profusion of bloom and color.

I have spoken of the rapid growth. The practical advantage of this as to fruit-trees is that one begins to have an income from them here sooner than in the East. No one need be under the delusion that he can live in California without work, or thrive without incessant and intelligent industry, but the distinction of the country for the fruit-grower is the rapidity with which trees and vines mature to the extent of being profitable. But nothing thrives without care, and kindly as the climate is to the weak, it cannot be too much insisted on that this is no place for confirmed invalids who have not money enough to live without work.

CHAPTER XIII.

THE immense county of San Diego is on the threshold of its development. It has comparatively only spots of cultivation here and there, in an area on the western slope of the county only, that Mr. Van Dyke estimates to contain about one million acres of good arable land for farming and fruit-raising. This mountainous region is full of charming valleys, and hidden among the hills are fruitful nooks capable of sustaining thriving communities. There is no doubt about the salubrity of the climate, and one can literally suit himself as to temperature by choosing his elevation. The traveller by rail down the wild Temecula Cañon will have some idea of the picturesqueness of the country, and, as he descends in the broadening valley, of the beautiful mountain parks of live-oak and clear running water, and of the richness both for grazing and grain of the ranches of the Santa Margarita, Las Flores, and Santa Rosa. Or if he will see what a few years of vigorous cultivation will do, he may visit Escondido, on the river of that name, which is at an elevation of less than a thousand feet, and fourteen miles from the ocean. This is only one of many settlements that have great natural beauty and thrifty industrial life. In that region are numerous attractive villages. I have a report from a little cañon, a few

SEXTON NURSERIES, NEAR SANTA BARBARA.

miles north of Escondido, where a
woman with an invalid husband
settled in 1883. The ground was thickly covered with brush, and its only
product was rabbits and quails. In
1888 they had 100 acres cleared and
fenced, mostly devoted to orchard
fruits and berries. They had in good
bearing over 1200 fruit-trees, among
them 200 oranges and 283 figs, which
yielded one and a half tons of figs a week during
the bearing season, from August to November. The
sprouts of the peach-trees grew twelve feet in 1889.
Of course such a little fruit farm as this is the result

of self-denial and hard work, but I am sure that the
experiment in this region need not be exceptional.

San Diego will be to the southern part of the State
what San Francisco is to the northern. Nature seems
to have arranged for this, by providing a magnificent
harbor, when it shut off the southern part by a mountain range. During the town-lot lunacy it was said
that San Diego could not grow because it had no back
country, and the retort was that it needed no back
country, its harbor would command commerce. The
fallacy of this assumption lay in the forgetfulness of
the fact that the profitable and peculiar exports of
Southern California must go East by rail, and reach a
market in the shortest possible time, and that the inhabitants look to the Pacific for comparatively little of
the imports they need. If the Isthmus route were
opened by a ship-canal, San Diego would doubtless
have a great share of the Pacific trade, and when the
population of that part of the State is large enough to
demand great importations from the islands and lands
of the Pacific, this harbor will not go begging. But
in its present development the entire Pacific trade of
Japan, China, and the islands, gives only a small divi-
dend each to the competing ports. For these develop-
ments this fine harbor must wait, but meantime the
wealth and prosperity of San Diego lie at its doors. A
country as large as the three richest New England
States, with enormous wealth of mineral and stone in
its mountains, with one of the finest climates in the
world, with a million acres of arable land, is certainly
capable of building up one great seaport town. These
million of acres on the western slope of the mountain
ranges of the country are geographically tributary to

San Diego, and almost every acre by its products is
certain to attain a high value.

The end of the ridiculous speculation in lots of
1887–88 was not so disastrous in the loss of money in-
vested, or even in the ruin of great expectations by the
collapse of fictitious values, as in the stoppage of im-
migration. The country has been ever since adjusting
itself to a normal growth, and the recovery is just in
proportion to the arrival of settlers who come to work
and not to speculate. I had heard that the "boom"
had left San Diego and vicinity the "deadest" region
to be found anywhere. A speculator would probably
so regard it. But the people have had a great accession of common-sense. The expectation of attracting
settlers by a fictitious show has subsided, and attention is directed to the development of the natural
riches of the country. Since the boom San Diego has
perfected a splendid system of drainage, paved its
streets, extended its railways, built up the business
part of the town solidly and handsomely, and greatly
improved the mesa above the town. In all essentials
of permanent growth it is much better in appearance
than in 1887. Business is better organized, and, best of
all, there is an intelligent appreciation of the agricultural resources of the country. It is discovered that
San Diego has a "back country" capable of producing
great wealth. The Chamber of Commerce has organized a permanent exhibition of products. It is assisted in this work of stimulation by competition by a
"Ladies' Annex," a society numbering some five hundred ladies, who devote themselves not to æsthetic
pursuits, but to the quickening of all the industries of
the farm and the garden, and all public improvements.

To the mere traveller who devotes only a couple of
weeks to an examination of this region it is evident
that the spirit of industry is in the ascendant, and the
result is a most gratifying increase in orchards and
vineyards, and the storage and distribution of water
for irrigation.   The region is unsurpassed for the production of the orange, the lemon, the raisin-grape, the
fig, and the olive.   The great reservoir of the Cuyamaca, which supplies San Diego, sends its flume
around the fertile valley of El Cajon (which has
already a great reputation for its raisins), and this has

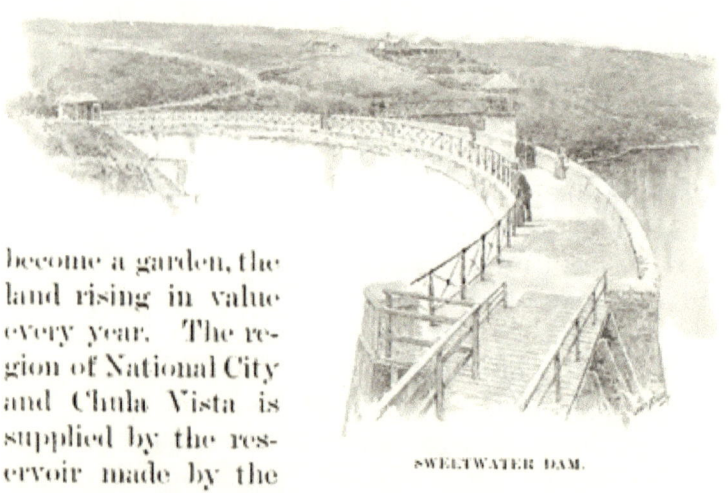

become a garden, the
land rising in value
every year.   The re-
gion of National City
and Chula Vista is
supplied by the res-
ervoir made by the
great Sweetwater

SWEETWATER DAM.

Dam—a marvel of engineering skill—and is not only
most productive in fruit, but is attractive by pretty

villas and most sightly and agreeable homes. It is an unanswerable reply to the inquiry if this region was not killed by the boom that all the arable land, except that staked out for fancy city prices, has steadily risen in value. This is true of all the bay region down through Otay (where a promising watch factory is established) to the border at Tia Juana. The rate of settlement in the county outside of the cities and towns has been greater since the boom than before—a most healthful indication for the future. According to the school census of 1889, Mr. Van Dyke estimates a permanent growth of nearly 50,000 people in the county in four years. Half of these are well distributed in small settlements which have the advantages of roads, mails, and school-houses, and which offer to settlers who wish to work adjacent unimproved land at prices which experience shows are still moderate.

10

CHAPTER XIV

A LAND OF AGREEABLE HOMES.

In this imperfect conspectus of a vast territory I should be sorry to say anything that can raise false expectations. Our country is very big; and though scarcely any part of it has not some advantages, and notwithstanding the census figures of our population, it will be a long time before our vast territory will fill up. California must wait with the rest; but it seems to me to have a great future. Its position in the Union with regard to its peculiar productions is unique. It can and will supply us with much that we now import, and labor and capital sooner or later will find their profit in meeting the growing demand for California products.

There are many people in the United States who could prolong life by moving to Southern California; there are many who would find life easier there by reason of the climate, and because out-door labor is more agreeable there the year through; many who have to fight the weather and a niggardly soil for existence could there have pretty little homes with less expense of money and labor. It is well that people for whom this is true should know it. It need not influence those who are already well placed to try the fortune of a distant country and new associations.

I need not emphasize the disadvantage in regard to

beauty of a land that can for half the year only keep
a vernal appearance by irrigation; but to eyes accustomed to it there is something pleasing in the contrast of the green valleys with the brown and gold and
red of the hills. The picture in my mind for the future of the Land of the Sun, of the mountains, of the
sea — which is only an enlargement of the picture of
the present—is one of great beauty. The rapid growth
of fruit and ornamental trees and the profusion of flowers render easy the making of a lovely home, however
humble it may be. The nature of the industries—requiring careful attention to a small piece of ground—
points to small holdings as a rule. The picture I see
is of a land of small farms and gardens, highly cultivated, in all the valleys and on the foot-hills; a land,
therefore, of luxuriance and great productiveness and
agreeable homes. I see everywhere the gardens, the
vineyards, the orchards, with the various greens of the
olive, the fig, and the orange. It is always picturesque,
because the country is broken and even rugged; it is
always interesting, because of the contrast with the
mountains and the desert; it has the color that makes
Southern Italy so poetic. It is the fairest field for the
experiment of a contented community, without any
poverty and without excessive wealth.

CHAPTER XV.

I WENT to it with reluctance. I shrink from attempting to say anything about it. If you knew that there was one spot on the earth where Nature kept her secret of secrets, the key to the action of her most gigantic and patient forces through the long eras, the marvel of constructive and destructive energy, in features of sublimity made possible to mental endurance by the most exquisite devices of painting and sculpture, the wonder which is without parallel or comparison, would you not hesitate to approach it? Would you not wander and delay with this and that wonder, and this and that beauty and nobility of scenery, putting off the day when the imagination, which is our highest gift, must be extinguished by the reality? The mind has this judicious timidity. Do we not loiter in the avenue of the temple, dallying with the vista of giant plane-trees and statues, and noting the carving and the color, mentally shrinking from the moment when the full glory shall burst upon us? We turn and look when we are near a summit, we pick a flower, we note the shape of the clouds, the passing breeze, before we take the last step that shall reveal to us the vast panorama of mountains and valleys.

I cannot bring myself to any description of the Grand Cañon of the Colorado by any other route, mental or physical, than that by which we reached it, by the way of such beauty as Monterey, such a wonder as the Yosemite, and the infinite and picturesque deserts of New Mexico and Arizona. I think the mind needs the training in the desert scenery to enable it to grasp the unique sublimity of the Grand Cañon.

The road to the Yosemite, after leaving the branch of the Southern Pacific at Raymond, is an unnecessarily fatiguing one. The journey by stage—sixty-five miles—is accomplished in less than two days—thirty-nine miles the first day, and twenty-six the second. The driving is necessarily slow, because two mountain ridges have to be surmounted, at an elevation each of about 6500 feet. The road is not a "road" at all as the term is understood in Switzerland, Spain, or in any highly civilized region—that is, a graded, smooth, hard, and sufficiently broad track. It is a makeshift highway, generally narrow (often too narrow for two teams to pass), cast up with loose material, or excavated on the slopes with frequent short curves and double curves. Like all mountain roads which skirt precipices, it may seem "pokerish," but it is safe enough if the drivers are skilful and careful (all the drivers on this route are not only excellent, but exceedingly civil as well), and there is no break in wagon or harness. At the season this trip is made the weather is apt to be warm, but this would not matter so much if the road were not intolerably dusty. Over a great part of the way the dust rises in clouds and is stifling. On a well-engineered road, with a good road-bed, the time of passage might not be shortened, but the journey would be made with positive comfort and enjoyment, for though there is a certain monotony in the scenery, there is the wild freshness of nature, now and then an extensive prospect, a sight of the snow-clad Nevadas, and vast stretches of woodland; and a part of the way the forests are magnificent, especially the stupendous growth of the sugar-pine. These noble forests are now protected by their inaccessibility.

From 1855 to 1864, nine years, the Yosemite had 653 visitors; in 1864 there were 147. The number increased steadily till 1869, the year the overland railroad was completed, when it jumped to 1122. Between 4000 and 5000 persons visit it now each year. The number would be enormously increased if it could be reached by rail, and doubtless a road will be built to the valley in the near future, perhaps up the Merced River. I believe that the pilgrims who used to go to the Yosemite on foot or on horseback regret the building of the stage road, the enjoyment of the wonderful valley being somehow cheapened by the comparative ease of reaching it. It is feared that a railway would still further cheapen, if it did not vulgarize it, and that passengers by train would miss the mountain scenery, the splendid forests, the surprises of the way (like the first view of the valley from Inspiration Point), and that the Mariposa big trees would be farther off the route than they are now. The traveller sees them now by driving eight miles from Wawona, the end of the first day's staging. But the romance for the few there is in staging will have to give way to the greater comfort of the many by

THE YOSEMITE DOME.

rail. The railway will do no more injury to the Yosemite than it has done to Niagara, and, in fact, will
be the means of immensely increasing the comfort of
the visitor's stay there, besides enabling tens of thousands of people to see it who cannot stand the fatigue
of the stage ride over the present road. The Yosemite
will remain as it is. The simplicity of its grand features is unassailable so long as the Government protects the forests that surround it and the streams that
pour into it. The visitor who goes there by rail will
find plenty of adventure for days and weeks in following the mountain trails, ascending to the great points
of view, exploring the cañons, or climbing so as to
command the vast stretch of the snowy Sierras. Or,
if he is not inclined to adventure, the valley itself will
satisfy his highest imaginative flights of the sublime
in rock masses and perpendicular ledges, and his sense
of beauty in the graceful water-falls, rainbow colors,
and exquisite lines of domes and pinnacles. It is in
the grouping of objects of sublimity and beauty that
the Yosemite excels. The narrow valley, with its
gigantic walls, which vary in every change of the
point of view, lends itself to the most astonishing
scenic effects, and these the photograph has repro-
duced, so that the world is familiar with the striking
features of the valley, and has a tolerably correct idea
of the sublimity of some of these features. What the
photograph cannot do is to give an impression of the
unique grouping, of the majesty, and at times crush-
ing weight upon the mind of the forms and masses,
of the atmospheric splendor and illusion, and of the
total value of such an assemblage of wonders. The
level surface of the peaceful, park-like valley has much

to do with the impression. The effect of El Capitan, seen across a meadow and rising from a beautiful park, is much greater than if it were encountered in a savage mountain gorge. The traveller may have seen elsewhere greater water-falls, and domes and spires of rock as surprising, but he has nowhere else seen such a combination as this. He may be fortified against surprise by the photographs he has seen and the reports of word painters, but he will not escape (say, at Inspiration Point, or Artist Point, or other lookouts), a quickening of the pulse and an elation which is physical as well as mental, in the sight of such unexpected sublimity and beauty. And familiarity will scarcely take off the edge of his delight, so varied are the effects in the passing hours and changing lights. The Rainbow Fall, when water is abundant, is exceedingly impressive as well as beautiful. Seen from the carriage road, pouring out of the sky overhead, it gives a sense of power, and at the proper hour before sunset, when the vast mass of leaping, foaming water is shot through with the colors of the spectrum, it is one of the most exquisite sights the world can offer; the elemental forces are overwhelming, but the loveliness is engaging. One turns from this to the noble mass of El Capitan with a shock of surprise, however often it may have been seen. This is the hour also, in the time of high-water, to see the reflection of the Yosemite Falls. As a spectacle it is infinitely finer than anything at Mirror Lake, and is unique in its way. To behold this beautiful series of falls, flowing down out of the blue sky above, and flowing up out of an equally blue sky in the depths of the earth, is a sight not to be forgotten.

And when the observer passes from these displays to
the sight of the aerial domes in the upper end of the
valley, new wonders opening at every turn of the forest road, his excitement has little chance of subsiding;
he may be even a little oppressed. The valley, so ver-

COAST OF MONTEREY

dant and friendly with grass and trees and flowers, is
so narrow compared with the height of its perpendicular guardian walls, and this little secluded spot is so
imprisoned in the gigantic mountains, that man has a
feeling of helplessness in it. This powerlessness in
the presence of elemental forces was heightened by
the deluge of water. There had been an immense fall
of snow the winter before, the Merced was a raging
torrent, overflowing its banks, and from every ledge
poured a miniature cataract.

Noble simplicity is the key-note to the scenery of
the Yosemite, and this is enhanced by the park-like
appearance of the floor of the valley. The stems of
the fine trees are in harmony with the perpendicular
lines, and their foliage adds the necessary contrast to
the gray rock masses. In order to preserve these for-

est-trees, the underbrush, which is liable to make a
conflagration in a dry season, should be removed generally, and the view of the great features be left unim-
peded. The minor cañons and the trails are, of course,
left as much as possible to the riot of vegetation. The
State Commission, which labors under the disadvantages of getting its supplies from a Legislature that
does not appreciate the value of the Yosemite to California, has developed the trails judiciously, and established a model trail service. The Yosemite, it need
not be said, is a great attraction to tourists from all
parts of the world; it is the interest of the State,
therefore, to increase their number by improving the

CYPRESS POINT.

facilities for reaching it, and by resolutely preserving
all the surrounding region from ravage

This is as true of the Mariposa big tree region as
of the valley   Indeed, more care is needed for the

trees than for the great chasm, for man cannot permanently injure the distinctive features of the latter, while the destruction of the sequoias will be an irreparable loss to the State and to the world. The *Sequoia gigantea* differs in leaf, and size and shape of cone, from

NEAR SEAL ROCK

the great *Sequoia semper virens* on the coast near Santa Cruz; neither can be spared. The Mariposa trees, scattered along on a mountain ridge 6500 feet above the sea, do not easily obtain their victory, for they are a part of a magnificent forest of other growths, among which the noble sugar-pine is conspicuous for its enormous size and graceful vigor. The sequoias dominate among splendid rivals only by a magnitude that has no comparison elsewhere in the world. I think no one can anticipate the effect that one of these monarchs will have upon him. He has read that a coach and six can drive through one of the trees that is standing: that another is thirty-three feet in diameter, and that its vast stem, 350 feet high, is crowned with a mass of foliage that seems to brush against the sky. He might be prepared for a tower 100 feet in circumference, and even 400 feet high, standing upon a level plain; but this living growth is quite another affair. Each tree is an individual, and has a personal character. No man can stand in the presence of one of these giants without a new sense of the age of the world and the insignificant span of one human life; but he is also overpowered by a sense of some gigantic personality. It does not relieve him to think of this as the Methuselah of trees, or to call it by the name of some great poet or captain. The awe the tree inspires is of itself. As one lies and looks up at the enormous bulk, it seems not so much the bulk, so lightly is it carried, as the spirit of the tree—the elastic vigor, the patience, the endurance of storm and change, the confident might, and the soaring, almost contemptuous pride, that overwhelm the puny spectator. It is just because man can measure himself, his littleness, his brevity of existence, with this growth out of the earth, that he is more personally impressed by it than he might be by the mere variation in the contour of the globe which is called a mountain. The imagination makes a plausible effort to comprehend it, and is foiled. No; clearly it is not mere size that impresses one; it is the dignity, the character in the tree, the authority and power of antiquity. Side by side of these venerable forms are young sequoias, great trees themselves, that have only just begun their millennial career—trees that will, if spared, perpetuate to remote ages this race of giants,

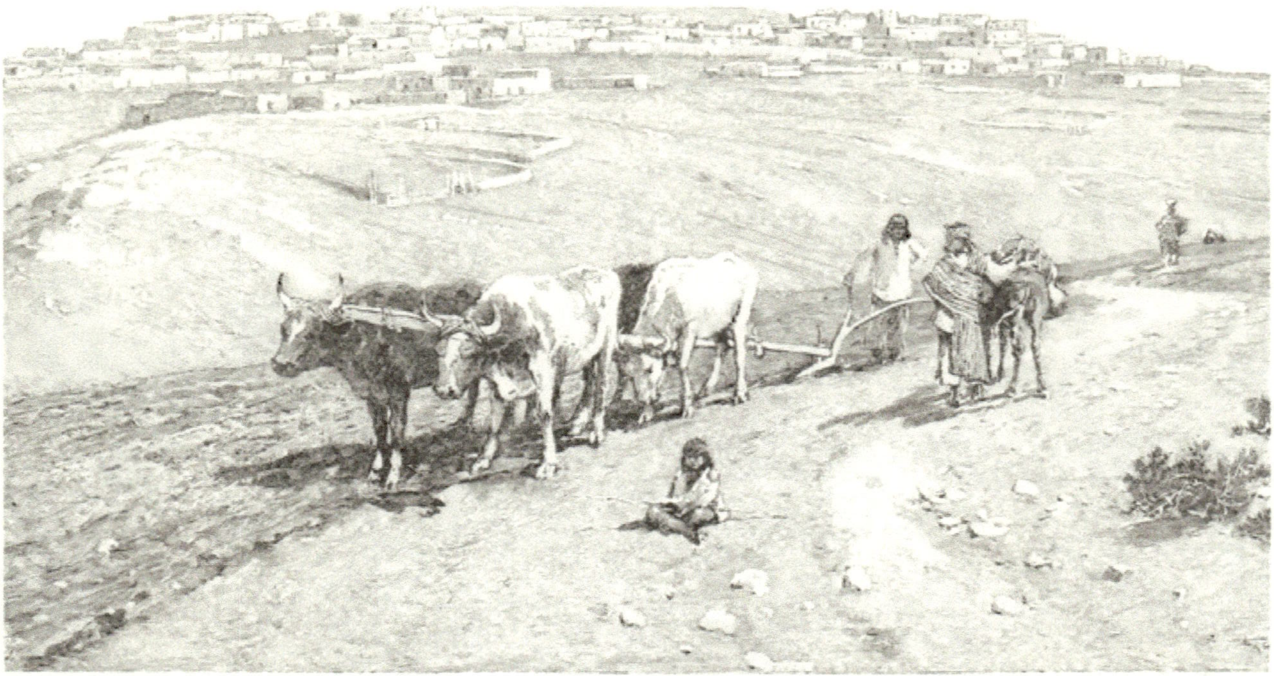

LAGUNA, FROM THE SOUTH-EAST.

and in two to four thousand years from now take the
place of their great-grandfathers, who are sinking under the weight of years, and one by one measuring
their length on the earth.

The transition from the sublime to the exquisitely
lovely in nature can nowhere else be made with more
celerity than from the Sierras to the coast at Monterey; California abounds in such contrasts and surprises. After the great stirring of the emotions by the
Yosemite and the Mariposa, the Hotel del Monte Park
and vicinity offer repose, and make an appeal to the
sense of beauty and refinement. Yet even here something unique is again encountered. I do not refer to
the extraordinary beauty of the giant live-oaks and
the landscape-gardening about the hotel, which have
made Monterey famous the world over, but to the sea-
beach drive of sixteen miles, which can scarcely be
rivalled elsewhere either for marine loveliness or variety of coast scenery. It has points like the ocean
drive at Newport, but is altogether on a grander scale,
and shows a more poetic union of shore and sea; besides, it offers the curious and fascinating spectacles
of the rocks inhabited by the sea-lions, and the Cypress Point. These huge, uncouth creatures can be
seen elsewhere, but probably nowhere else on this
coast are they massed in greater numbers. The trees
of Cypress Point are unique, this species of cypress
having been found nowhere else. The long, never-
ceasing swell of the Pacific incessantly flows up the
many crescent sand beaches, casting up shells of brilliant hues, sea-weed, and kelp, which seems instinct
with animal life, and flotsam from the far-off islands.
But the rocks that lie off the shore, and the jagged
11

points that project in fanciful forms, break the even
great swell, and send the waters, churned into spray
and foam, into the air with a thousand hues in the
sun.   The shock of these sharp collisions mingles
with the heavy ocean boom.   Cypress Point is one
of the most conspicuous of these projections, and its
strange trees creep out upon the ragged ledges almost
to the water's edge.   These cypresses are quite as instinct with individual life and quite as fantastic as
any that Doré drew for his " Inferno."   They are as
gnarled and twisted as olive-trees two centuries old,
but their attitudes seem not only to show struggle
with the elements, but agony in that struggle.   The
agony may be that of torture in the tempest, or of
some fabled creatures fleeing and pursued, stretching
out their long arms in terror, and fixed in that writh-
ing fear.   They are creatures of the sea quite as much
as of the land, and they give to this lovely coast a
strange charm and fascination.

CHAPTER XVI

THE traveller to California by the Santa Fé route
comes into the arid regions gradually, and finds each
day a variety of objects of interest that upsets his
conception of a monotonous desert land. If he chooses
to break the continental journey midway, he can turn
aside at Las Vegas to the Hot Springs. Here, at the
head of a picturesque valley, is the Montezuma Hotel, a luxurious and handsome house, 6767 feet above
sea-level, a great surprise in the midst of the broken
and somewhat savage New Mexican scenery. The
low hills covered with pines and piñons, the romantic
glens, and the wide views from the elevations about
the hotel, make it an attractive place; and a great
deal has been done, in the erection of bath-houses,
ornamental gardening, and the grading of roads and
walks, to make it a comfortable place. The latitude
and the dryness of the atmosphere insure for the traveller from the North in our winter an agreeable recep-
tion, and the elevation makes the spot in the summer
a desirable resort from Southern heat. It is a sanita-
rium as well as a pleasure resort. The Hot Springs
have much the same character as the Töplitz waters in
Bohemia, and the saturated earth—the *Mütterlager*—
furnishes the curative "mud baths" which are enjoyed
at Marienbad and Carlsbad. The union of the climate,

which is so favorable in diseases of the respiratory organs, with the waters, which do so much for rheumatic sufferers, gives a distinction to Las Vegas Hot Springs. This New Mexican air—there is none purer on the globe—is an enemy to hay-fever and malarial diseases. It was a wise enterprise to provide that those who wish to try its efficacy can do so at the Montezuma without giv-

CHURCH AT LAGUNA.

ing up any of the comforts of civilized life.

It is difficult to explain to one who has not seen it, or will not put himself in the leisurely frame of mind to enjoy it, the charms of the desert of the high plateaus of New Mexico and Arizona. Its arid character is not so impressive as its ancientness; and the part which interests us is not only the procession of the long geologic eras, visible in the extinct volcanoes, the

barrancas, the painted buttes, the petrified forests, but
as well in the evidences of civilizations gone by, or the
remains of them surviving in our day—the cliff dwellings, the ruins of cities that were thriving when Coronado sent his lieutenants through the region three
centuries ago, and the present residences of the Pueblo Indians, either villages perched upon an almost inaccessible rock like Acamo, or clusters of adobe dwellings like Isleta and Laguna. The Pueblo Indians, of
whom the Zuñis are a tribe, have been dwellers in villages and cultivators of the soil and of the arts of
peace immemorially, a gentle, amiable race. It is indeed such a race as one would expect to find in the
land of the sun and the cactus. Their manners and
their arts attest their antiquity and a long refinement
in fixed dwellings and occupations. The whole region
is a most interesting field for the antiquarian.

We stopped one day at Laguna, which is on the
Santa Fé line west of Isleta, another Indian pueblo
at the Atlantic and Pacific junction, where the road
crosses the Rio Grande del Norte west of Albuquer-
que. Near Laguna a little stream called the Rio Puer-
co flows southward and joins the Rio Grande. There
is verdure along these streams, and gardens and fruit
orchards repay the rude irrigation. In spite of these
watercourses the aspect of the landscape is wild and
desert-like—low barren hills and ragged ledges, wide
sweeps of sand and dry gray bushes, with mountains
and long lines of horizontal ledges in the distance.
Laguna is built upon a rounded elevation of rock.
Its appearance is exactly that of a Syrian village, the
same cluster of little, square, flat-roofed houses in terraces, the same brown color, and under the same pale
11*

blue sky. And the resemblance was completed by the
figures of the women on the roofs, or moving down
the slope, erect and supple, carrying on the head a
water jar, and holding together by one hand the mantle worn like a Spanish *rebozo*. The village is irregularly built, without much regard to streets or alleys,
and it has no special side of entrance or approach.
Every side presents a blank wall of adobe, and the entrance seems quite by chance. Yet the way we went
over, the smooth slope was worn here and there in
channels three or four inches deep, as if by the passing feet of many generations. The only semblance of
architectural regularity is in the plaza, not perfectly
square, upon which some of the houses look, and
where the annual dances take place. The houses
have the effect of being built in terraces rising one
above the other, but it is hard to say exactly what a
house is—whether it is anything more than one room.
You can reach some of the houses only by aid of a
ladder. You enter others from the street. If you will
go farther you must climb a ladder which brings you
to the roof that is used as the sitting-room or door-
yard of the next room. From this room you may still
ascend to others, or you may pass through low and
small door-ways to other apartments. It is all hap-
hazard, but exceedingly picturesque. You may find
some of the family in every room, or they may be
gathered, women and babies, on a roof which is protected by a parapet. At the time of our visit the men
were all away at work in their fields. Notwithstanding the houses are only sun-dried bricks, and the village is without water or street commissioners, I was
struck by the universal cleanliness. There was no ref-

TERRACED HOUSES, PUEBLO OF LAGUNA.

use in the corners or alleys, no odors, and many of the
rooms were patterns of neatness.   To be sure, an old
woman here and there kept her hens in an adjoining
apartment above her own, and there was the litter of
children and of rather careless house - keeping.   But,
taken altogether, the town is an example for some

more civilized, whose inhabitants wash oftener and dress better than these Indians.

We were put on friendly terms with the whole settlement through three or four young maidens who had been at the Carlisle school, and spoke English very prettily. They were of the ages of fifteen and sixteen, and some of them had been five years away. They came back, so far as I could learn, gladly to their own people and to the old ways. They had resumed the Indian dress, which is much more becoming to them, as I think they know, than that which had been imposed upon them. I saw no books. They do not read any now, and they appear to be perfectly content with the idle drudgery of their semi-savage condition. In time they will marry in their tribe, and the school episode will be a thing of the past. But not altogether. The pretty Josephine, who was our best cicerone about the place, a girl of lovely eyes and modest mien, showed us with pride her own room, or "house," as she called it, neat as could be, simply furnished with an iron bedstead and snow-white cot, a mirror, chair, and table, and a trunk, and some "advertising" prints on the walls. She said that she was needed at home to cook for her aged mother, and her present ambition was to make money enough by the sale of pottery and curios to buy a cooking stove, so that she could cook more as the whites do. The house-work of the family had mainly fallen upon her; but it was not burdensome, I fancied, and she and the other girls of her age had leisure to go to the station on the arrival of every train, in hope of selling something to the passengers, and to sit on the rocks in the sun and dream as maidens do. I fancy it would be

better for Josephine and for all the rest if there were
no station and no passing trains. The elder women
were uniformly ugly, but not repulsive like the Mo-
javes; the place swarmed with children, and the babies, aged women, and pleasing young girls grouped
most effectively on the roofs.

The whole community were very complaisant and
friendly when we came to know them well, which we
did in the course of an hour, and they enjoyed as
much as we did the bargaining for pottery. They
have for sale a great quantity of small pieces, fantastic
in form and brilliantly colored—toys, in fact; but we
found in their houses many beautiful jars of large size
and excellent shape, decorated most effectively. The
ordinary utensils for cooking and for cooling water
are generally pretty in design and painted artistically.
Like the ancient Peruvians, they make many vessels
in the forms of beasts and birds. Some of the designs
of the decoration are highly conventionalized, and
others are just in the proper artistic line of the natural—a spray with a bird, or a sunflower on its stalk.
The ware is all unglazed, exceedingly light and thin,
and baked so hard that it has a metallic sound when
struck. Some of the large jars are classic in shape,
and recall in form and decoration the ancient Cypriote
ware, but the colors are commonly brilliant and bar-
baric. The designs seem to be indigenous, and to be-
tray little Spanish influence. The art displayed in
this pottery is indeed wonderful, and, to my eye, much
more effective and lastingly pleasing than much of
our cultivated decoration. A couple of handsome jars
that I bought of an old woman, she assured me she
made and decorated herself; but I saw no ovens there,

nor any signs of manufacture, and suppose that most of the ware is made at Acoma.

It did not seem to be a very religious community, although the town has a Catholic church, and I understand that Protestant services are sometimes held in the place. The church is not much frequented, and the only evidence of devotion I encountered was in a woman who wore a large and handsome silver cross, made by the Navajos. When I asked its price, she clasped it to her bosom, with an upward look full of faith and of refusal to part with her religion at any price. The church, which is adobe, and at least two centuries old, is one of the most interesting I have seen anywhere. It is a simple parallelogram, 104 feet long and 21 feet broad, the gable having an opening in which the bells hang. The interior is exceedingly curious, and its decorations are worth reproduction. The floor is of earth, and many of the tribe who were distinguished and died long ago are said to repose under its smooth surface, with nothing to mark their place of sepulture. It has an open timber roof, the beams supported upon carved corbels. The ceiling is made of wooden sticks, about two inches in diameter and some four feet long, painted in alternated colors— red, blue, orange, and black—and so twisted or woven together as to produce the effect of plaited straw, a most novel and agreeable decoration. Over the entrance is a small gallery, the under roof of which is composed of sticks laid in straw pattern and colored. All around the wall runs a most striking dado, an odd, angular pattern, with conventionalized birds at intervals, painted in strong yet *fade* colors—red, yellow, black, and white. The north wall is without win-

dows: all the light, when the door is closed, comes from two irregular windows, without glass, high up in the south wall. The chancel walls are covered with frescos, and there are several quaint paintings, some of them not very bad in color and drawing. The altar, which is supported at the sides by twisted wooden pillars, carved with a knife, is hung with ancient sheepskins brightly painted. Back of the altar are some archaic wooden images, colored; and over the altar, on the ceiling, are the stars of heaven, and the sun and the moon, each with a face in it. The interior was scrupulously clean and sweet and restful to one coming in from the glare of the sun on the desert. It was evidently little used, and the Indians who accompanied us seemed under no strong impression of its sanctity; but we liked to linger in it, it was so *bizarre*, so picturesque, and exhibited in its rude decoration so much taste. Two or three small birds flitting about seemed to enjoy the coolness and the subdued light, and were undisturbed by our presence.

These are children of the desert, kin in their condition and the influences that formed them to the sedentary tribes of upper Egypt and Arabia, who pitch their villages upon the rocky eminences, and depend for subsistence upon irrigation and scant pasturage. Their habits are those of the dwellers in an arid land which has little in common with the wilderness—the inhospitable northern wilderness of rain and frost and snow. Rain, to be sure, insures some sort of vegetation in the most forbidding and intractable country, but that does not save the harsh landscape from being unattractive. The high plateaus of New Mexico and Arizona have everything that the rainy wilderness

INTERIOR OF THE CHURCH AT LAGUNA.

lacks—sunshine, heaven's own air, immense breadth of horizon, color and infinite beauty of outline, and a warm soil with unlimited possibilities when moistened. All that these deserts need is water. A fatal want? No. That is simply saying that science can do for this region what it cannot do for the high wilderness of frost—by the transportation of water transform it

into gardens of bloom and fields of fruitfulness. The
wilderness shall be made to feed the desert.

I confess that these deserts in the warm latitudes
fascinate me. Perhaps it is because I perceive in
them such a chance for the triumph of the skill of
man, seeing how, here and there, his energy has pushed
the desert out of his path across the continent. But
I fear that I am not so practical. To many the desert in its stony sterility, its desolateness, its unbroken
solitude, its fantastic savageness, is either appalling or
repulsive. To them it is tiresome and monotonous.
The vast plains of Kansas and Nebraska are monotonous even in the agricultural green of summer. Not
so to me the desert. It is as changeable in its lights
and colors as the ocean. It is even in its general features of sameness never long the same. If you trav-
erse it on foot or on horseback, there is ever some minor novelty. And on the swift train, if you draw down
the curtain against the glare, or turn to your book,
you are sure to miss something of interest — a deep
cañon rift in the plain, a turn that gives a wide view
glowing in a hundred hues in the sun, a savage gorge
with beetling rocks, a solitary butte or red truncated
pyramid thrust up into the blue sky, a horizontal ledge
cutting the horizon line as straight as a ruler for miles,
a pointed cliff uplifted sheer from the plain and laid in
regular courses of Cyclopean masonry, the battlements
of a fort, a terraced castle with towers and esplanade,
a great trough of a valley, gray and parched, enclosed
by far purple mountains. And then the unlimited
freedom of it, its infinite expansion, its air like wine
to the senses, the floods of sunshine, the waves of
color, the translucent atmosphere that aids the im-

agination to create in the distance all architectural
splendors and realms of peace. It is all like a mirage
and a dream. We pass swiftly, and make a moving
panorama of beauty in hues, of strangeness in forms,
of sublimity in extent, of overawing and savage antiquity. I would miss none of it. And when we pass to
the accustomed again, to the fields of verdure and the
forests and the hills of green, and are limited in view
and shut in by that which we love, after all, better
than the arid land, I have a great longing to see again
the desert, to be a part of its vastness, and to feel
once more the freedom and inspiration of its illimita-
ble horizons.

CHAPTER XVII.

THE HEART OF THE DESERT.

THERE is an arid region lying in Northern Arizona and Southern Utah which has been called the District of the Grand Cañon of the Colorado. The area, roughly estimated, contains from 13,000 to 16,000 square miles—about the size of the State of Maryland. This region, fully described by the explorers and studied by the geologists in the United States service, but little known to even the travelling public, is probably the most interesting territory of its size on the globe. At least it is unique. In attempting to convey an idea of it the writer can be assisted by no comparison, nor can he appeal in the minds of his readers to any experience of scenery that can apply here. The so-called Grand Cañon differs not in degree from all other scenes; it differs in kind.

The Colorado River flows southward through Utah, and crosses the Arizona line below the junction with the San Juan. It continues southward, flowing deep in what is called the Marble Cañon, till it is joined by the Little Colorado, coming up from the south-east; it then turns westward in a devious line until it drops straight south, and forms the western boundary of Arizona. The centre of the district mentioned is the westwardly flowing part of the Colorado. South of the river is the Colorado Plateau, at a general eleva-

12

tion of about 7000 feet. North of it the land is higher, and ascends in a series of plateaus, and then terraces, a succession of cliffs like a great stair-way, rising to the high plateaus of Utah. The plateaus, adjoining the river on the north and well marked by north and south dividing lines, or faults, are, naming them from east to west, the Paria, the Kaibab, the Kanab, the Uinkaret, and the Sheavwitz, terminating in a great wall on the west, the Great Wash fault, where the surface of the country drops at once from a general elevation of 6000 feet to from 1300 to 3000 feet above the sea-level—into a desolate and formidable desert.

If the Grand Cañon itself did not dwarf everything else, the scenery of these plateaus would be superlative in interest. It is not all desert, nor are the gorges, cañons, cliffs, and terraces, which gradually prepare the mind for the comprehension of the Grand Cañon, the only wonders of this land of enchantment. These are contrasted with the sylvan scenery of the Kaibab Plateau, its giant forests and parks, and broad meadows decked in the summer with wild flowers in dense masses of scarlet, white, purple, and yellow. The Vermilion Cliffs, the Pink Cliffs, the White Cliffs, surpass in fantastic form and brilliant color anything that the imagination conceives possible in nature, and there are dreamy landscapes quite beyond the most exquisite fancies of Claude and of Turner. The region is full of wonders, of beauties, and sublimities that Shelley's imaginings do not match in the "Prometheus Unbound," and when it becomes accessible to the tourist it will offer an endless field for the delight of those whose minds can rise to the heights of the sublime and the beautiful. In all imaginative writing

or painting the material used is that of human experience, otherwise it could not be understood; even heaven must be described in the terms of an earthly paradise. Human experience has no prototype of this region, and the imagination has never conceived of its forms and colors. It is impossible to convey an adequate idea of it by pen or pencil or brush. The reader who is familiar with the glowing descriptions in the official reports of Major J. W. Powell, Captain C. E. Dutton, Lieutenant Ives, and others, will not save himself from a shock of surprise when the reality is before him. This paper deals only with a single view in this marvellous region.

The point where we struck the Grand Cañon, approaching it from the south, is opposite the promontory in the Kaibab Plateau named Point Sublime by Major Powell, just north of the 36th parallel, and 112° 15′ west longitude. This is only a few miles west of the junction with the Little Colorado. About three or four miles west of this junction the river enters the east slope of the east Kaibab monocline, and here the Grand Cañon begins. Rapidly the chasm deepens to about 6000 feet, or rather it penetrates a higher country, the slope of the river remaining about the same. Through this lofty plateau—an elevation of 7000 to 9000 feet—the chasm extends for sixty miles, gradually changing its course to the north-west, and entering the Kanab Plateau. The Kaibab division of the Grand Cañon is by far the sublimest of all, being 1000 feet deeper than any other. It is not grander only on account of its greater depth, but it is broader and more diversified with magnificent architectural features.

12*

The Kanab division, only less magnificent than the Kaibab, receives the Kanab Cañon from the north and the Cataract Cañon from the south, and ends at the Toroweap Valley.

The section of the Grand Cañon seen by those who take the route from Peach Springs is between 113 and 114° west longitude, and, though wonderful, presents few of the great features of either the Kaibab or the Kanab divisions. The Grand Cañon ends, west longitude 114°, at the Great Wash, west of the Hurricane Ledge or Fault. Its whole length from Little Colorado to the Great Wash, measured by the meanderings of the surface of the river, is 220 miles; by a median line between the crests of the summits of the walls with two-mile cords, about 195 miles; the distance in a straight line is 125 miles.

In our journey to the Grand Cañon we left the Santa Fé line at Flagstaff, a new town with a lively lumber industry, in the midst of a spruce-pine forest which occupies the broken country through which the road passes for over fifty miles. The forest is open, the trees of moderate size are too thickly set with low-growing limbs to make clean lumber, and the foliage furnishes the minimum of shade; but the change to these woods is a welcome one from the treeless reaches of the desert on either side. The cañon is also reached from Williams, the next station west, the distance being a little shorter, and the point on the cañon visited being usually a little farther west. But the Flagstaff route is for many reasons usually preferred. Flagstaff lies just south-east of the San Francisco Mountain, and on the great Colorado Plateau, which has a pretty uniform elevation of about 7000 feet above the sea. The whole region is full of interest. Some of the most remarkable cliff dwellings are within ten miles of Flagstaff, on the Walnut Creek

TOURISTS IN THE COLORADO CAÑON.

Cañon. At Holbrook, 100 miles east, the traveller finds a road some forty miles long, that leads to the great petrified forest, or Chalcedony Park. Still farther east are the villages of the Pueblo Indians, near the line, while to the northward is the great reservation of the Navajos, a nomadic tribe celebrated for its fine blankets and pretty work in silver—a tribe

that preserves much of its manly independence by
shunning the charity of the United States. No Indians have come into intimate or dependent relations
with the whites without being deteriorated.

Flagstaff is the best present point of departure, because it has a small hotel, good supply stores, and a
large livery-stable, made necessary by the business of
the place and the objects of interest in the neighborhood, and because one reaches from there by the easi-
est road the finest scenery incomparably on the Colorado. The distance is seventy-six miles through a
practically uninhabited country, much of it a desert,
and with water very infrequent. No work has been
done on the road; it is made simply by driving over
it. There are a few miles here and there of fair wheel-
ing, but a good deal of it is intolerably dusty or exceedingly stony, and progress is slow. In the daytime
(it was the last of June) the heat is apt to be excessive; but this could be borne, the air is so absolutely
dry and delicious, and breezes occasionally spring up,
if it were not for the dust. It is, notwithstanding the
novelty of the adventure and of the scenery by the
way, a tiresome journey of two days. A day of rest is
absolutely required at the cañon, so that five days
must be allowed for the trip. This will cost the traveller, according to the size of the party made up, from
forty to fifty dollars. But a much longer sojourn at
the cañon is desirable.

Our party of seven was stowed in and on an old
Concord coach drawn by six horses, and piled with
camp equipage, bedding, and provisions. A four-horse
team followed, loaded with other supplies and cooking
utensils. The road lies on the east side of the San

Francisco Mountain. Returning, we passed around its west side, gaining thus a complete view of this shapely peak. The compact range is a group of extinct volcanoes, the craters of which are distinctly visible. The cup-like summit of the highest is 13,000 feet above the sea, and snow always lies on the north escarpment. Rising about 6000 feet above the point of view of the great plateau, it is from all sides a noble object, the dark rock, snow-sprinkled, rising out of the dense growth of pine and cedar. We drove at first through open pine forests, through park-like intervals, over the foot-hills of the mountain, through growths of scrub cedar, and out into the ever-varying rolling country to widely-extended prospects. Two considerable hills on our right attracted us by their unique beauty. Upon the summit and side of each was a red glow exactly like the tint of sunset. We thought surely that it was the effect of reflected light, but the sky was cloudless and the color remained constant. The color came from the soil. The first was called Sunset Mountain. One of our party named the other, and the more beautiful, Peachblow Mountain, a poetic and perfectly descriptive name.

We lunched at noon beside a swift, clouded, cold stream of snow-water from the San Francisco, along which grew a few gnarled cedars and some brilliant wild flowers. The scene was more than picturesque: in the clear hot air of the desert the distant landscape made a hundred pictures of beauty. Behind us the dark form of San Francisco rose up 6000 feet to its black crater and fields of spotless snow. Away off to the north-east, beyond the brown and gray pastures, across a far line distinct in dull color, lay the Painted

Desert, like a mirage, like a really painted landscape,
glowing in red and orange and pink, an immense city
rather than a landscape, with towers and terraces and
façades, melting into indistinctness as in a rosy mist,
spectral but constant, weltering in a tropic glow and
heat, walls and columns and shafts, the wreck of an
Oriental capital on a wide violet plain, suffused with
brilliant color softened into exquisite shades. All over
this region nature has such surprises, that laugh at
our inadequate conception of her resources.

Our camp for the night was at the next place
where water could be obtained, a station of the Arizona Cattle Company. Abundant water is piped down
to it from mountain springs. The log-house and sta-
ble of the cow-boys were unoccupied, and we pitched
our tent on a knoll by the corral. The night was absolutely dry, and sparkling with the starlight. A part
of the company spread their blankets on the ground
under the sky. It is apt to be cold in this region
towards morning, but lodging in the open air is no
hardship in this delicious climate. The next day the
way part of the distance, with only a road marked
by wagon wheels, was through extensive and barren-
looking cattle ranges, through pretty vales of grass
surrounded by stunted cedars, and over stormy ridges
and plains of sand and small bowlders. The water
having failed at Red Horse, the only place where it is
usually found in the day's march, our horses went
without, and we had resource to our canteens. The
whole country is essentially arid, but snow falls in the
winter-time, and its melting, with occasional showers
in the summer, create what are called surface wells,
made by drainage. Many of them go dry by June.

There had been no rain in the region since the last of
March, but clouds were gathering daily, and showers
are always expected in July. The phenomenon of
rain on this baked surface, in this hot air, and with
this immense horizon, is very interesting. Showers in
this tentative time are local. In our journey we saw
showers far off, we experienced a dash for ten minutes, but it was local, covering not more than a mile or
two square. We have in sight a vast canopy of blue
sky, of forming and dispersing clouds. It is difficult
for them to drop their moisture in the rising columns
of hot air. The result at times was a very curious
spectacle — rain in the sky that did not reach the
earth. Perhaps some cold current high above us
would condense the moisture, which would begin to
fall in long trailing sweeps, blown like fine folds of
muslin, or like sheets of dissolving sugar, and then the
hot air of the earth would dissipate it, and the showers
would be absorbed in the upper regions. The heat
was sometimes intense, but at intervals a refreshing
wind would blow, the air being as fickle as the rain;
and now and then we would see a slender column of
dust, a thousand or two feet high, marching across the
desert, apparently not more than two feet in diameter,
and wavering like the threads of moisture that tried in
vain to reach the earth as rain. Of life there was not
much to be seen in our desert route. In the first day
we encountered no habitation except the ranch-house
mentioned, and saw no human being; and the second
day none except the solitary occupant of the dried
well at Red Horse, and two or three Indians on the
hunt. A few squirrels were seen, and a rabbit now
and then, and occasionally a bird. The general im-

pression was that of a deserted land. But antelope
abound in the timber regions, and we saw several of
these graceful creatures quite near us. Excellent antelope steaks, bought of the wandering Indian hunters,
added something to our "canned" supplies. One day
as we lunched, without water, on the cedar slope of a
lovely grass interval, we saw coming towards us over
the swells of the prairie a figure of a man on a horse.
It rode to us straight as the crow flies. The Indian
pony stopped not two feet from where our group sat,
and the rider, who was an Oualapai chief, clad in sack-
ing, with the print of the brand of flour or salt on his
back, dismounted with his Winchester rifle, and stood
silently looking at us without a word of salutation.
He stood there, impassive, until we offered him something to eat. Having eaten all we gave him, he opened his mouth and said, "Smoke 'em!" Having pro-
cured from the other wagon a pipe of tobacco and
a pull at the driver's canteen, he returned to us all
smiles. His only baggage was the skull of an antelope, with the horns, hung at his saddle. Into this he
put the bread and meat which we gave him, mounted
the wretched pony, and without a word rode straight
away. At a little distance he halted, dismounted, and
motioned towards the edge of the timber, where he
had spied an antelope. But the game eluded him, and
he mounted again and rode off across the desert—a
strange figure. His tribe lives in the cañon some fifty
miles west, and was at present encamped, for the purpose of hunting, in the pine woods not far from the
point we were aiming at.

CHAPTER XVIII.

ON THE BRINK OF THE GRAND CAÑON.—THE UNIQUE MARVEL OF NATURE.

THE way seemed long. With the heat and dust and slow progress, it was exceedingly wearisome. Our modern nerves are not attuned to the slow crawling of a prairie-wagon. There had been growing for some time in the coach a feeling that the journey did not pay; that, in fact, no mere scenery could compensate for the fatigue of the trip. The imagination did not rise to it. "It will have to be a very big cañon," said the duchess.

Late in the afternoon we entered an open pine forest, passed through a meadow where the Indians had set their camp by a shallow pond, and drove along a ridge, in the cool shades, for three or four miles. Suddenly, on the edge of a descent, we who were on the box saw through the tree-tops a vision that stopped the pulse for a second, and filled us with excitement. It was only a glimpse, far off and apparently lifted up—red towers, purple cliffs, wide-spread apart, hints of color and splendor; on the right distance, mansions, gold and white and carmine (so the light made them), architectural habitations in the sky it must be, and suggestions of others far off in the middle distance—a substantial aerial city, or the ruins of one, such as the prophet saw in a vision. It was only

a glimpse. Our hearts were in our mouths. We had
a vague impression of something wonderful, fearful
—some incomparable splendor that was not earthly.
Were we drawing near the "City?" and should we
have yet a more perfect view thereof? Was it Jerusalem or some Hindoo temples there in the sky? "It
was builded of pearls and precious stones, also the
streets were paved with gold; so that by reason of
the natural glory of the city, and the reflection of the
sunbeams upon it, Christian with desire fell sick." It
was a momentary vision of a vast amphitheatre of
splendor, mostly hidden by the trees and the edge of
the plateau.

We descended into a hollow. There was the well,
a log-cabin, a tent or two under the pine-trees. We
dismounted with impatient haste. The sun was low
in the horizon, and had long withdrawn from this
grassy dell. Tired as we were, we could not wait. It
was only to ascend the little steep, stony slope—300
yards—and we should see! Our party were straggling
up the hill; two or three had reached the edge. I
looked up. The duchess threw up her arms and
screamed. We were not fifteen paces behind, but we
saw nothing. We took the few steps, and the whole
magnificence broke upon us. No one could be prepared for it. The scene is one to strike dumb with
awe, or to unstring the nerves; one might stand in
silent astonishment, another would burst into tears.

There are some experiences that cannot be repeated—one's first view of Rome, one's first view of Jerusalem. But these emotions are produced by associ-
ation, by the sudden standing face to face with the
scenes most wrought into our whole life and educa-

GRAND CAÑON OF THE COLORADO—VIEW FROM THE HANCE TRAIL.

tion by tradition and religion. This was without as-
sociation, as it was without parallel. It was a shock
so novel that the mind, dazed, quite failed to comprehend it. All that we could grasp was a vast confusion of amphitheatres and strange architectural forms
resplendent with color. The vastness of the view
amazed us quite as much as its transcendent beauty.

We had expected a cañon—two lines of perpendicular walls 6000 feet high, with the ribbon of a river
at the bottom; but the reader may dismiss all his no-
tions of a cañon, indeed of any sort of mountain or
gorge scenery with which he is familiar. We had come
into a new world. What we saw was not a cañon, or
a chasm, or a gorge, but a vast area which is a break
in the plateau. From where we stood it was twelve
miles across to the opposite walls—a level line of
mesa on the Utah side. We looked up and down for
twenty to thirty miles. This great space is filled with
gigantic architectural constructions, with amphitheatres, gorges, precipices, walls of masonry, fortresses
terraced up to the level of the eye, temples mountain
size, all brilliant with horizontal lines of color—streaks
of solid hues a few feet in width, streaks a thousand
feet in width—yellows, mingled white and gray, orange,
dull red, brown, blue, carmine, green, all blending in
the sunlight into one transcendent suffusion of splendor. Afar off we saw the river in two places, a mere
thread, as motionless and smooth as a strip of mirror,
only we knew it was a turbid, boiling torrent, 6000
feet below us. Directly opposite the overhanging
ledge on which we stood was a mountain, the sloping
base of which was ashy gray and bluish; it rose in a
series of terraces to a thousand-feet wall of dark red

13

sandstone, receding upward, with ranges of columns and many fantastic sculptures, to a finial row of gigantic opera-glasses 6000 feet above the river. The great San Francisco Mountain, with its snowy crater, which we had passed on the way, might have been set down in the place of this one, and it would have been only one in a multitude of such forms that met the eye whichever way we looked. Indeed, all the vast mountains in this region might be hidden in this cañon.

Wandering a little away from the group and out of sight, and turning suddenly to the scene from another point of view, I experienced for a moment an indescribable terror of nature, a confusion of mind, a fear to be alone in such a presence. With all this grotesqueness and majesty of form and radiance of color, creation seemed in a whirl. With our education in scenery of a totally different kind, I suppose it would need long acquaintance with this to familiarize one with it to the extent of perfect mental comprehension.

The vast abyss has an atmosphere of its own, one always changing and producing new effects, an atmosphere and shadows and tones of its own—golden, rosy, gray, brilliant, and sombre, and playing a thousand fantastic tricks to the vision. The rich and wonderful color effects, says Captain Dutton, "are due to the inherent colors of the rocks, modified by the atmosphere. Like any other great series of strata in the plateau province, the carboniferous has its own range of colors, which might serve to distinguish it, even if we had no other criterion. The summit strata are pale gray, with a faint yellowish cast. Beneath them the cross-bedded sandstone appears, showing a mottled

surface of pale pinkish hue. Underneath this member
are nearly 1000 feet of the lower Aubrey sandstones,
displaying an intensely brilliant red, which is somewhat marked by the talus shot down from the gray
cherty limestone at the summit. Beneath the lower
Aubrey is the face of the Red Wall limestone, from
2000 to 3000 feet high. It has a strong red tone, but
a very peculiar one. Most of the red strata of the
West have the brownish or vermilion tones, but these
are rather purplish red, as if the pigment had been
treated to a dash of blue. It is not quite certain that
this may not arise in part from the intervention of
the blue haze, and probably it is rendered more conspicuous by this cause; but, on the whole, the purplish cast seems to be inherent. This is the domi-
nant color of the cañon, for the expanse of the rock
surface displayed is more than half in the Red Wall
group."

I was continually likening this to a vast city rather
than a landscape, but it was a city of no man's creation nor of any man's conception. In the visions
which inspired or crazy painters have had of the New
Jerusalem, of Babylon the Great, of a heaven in the
atmosphere, with endless perspective of towers and
steeps that hang in the twilight sky, the imagination
has tried to reach this reality. But here are effects
beyond the artist, forms the architect has not hinted
at; and yet everything reminds us of man's work.
And the explorers have tried by the use of Oriental
nomenclature to bring it within our comprehension,
the East being the land of the imagination. There
is the Hindoo Amphitheatre, the Bright Angel Amphitheatre, the Ottoman Amphitheatre, Shiva's Tem-

ple, Vishnu's Temple, Vulcan's Throne. And here, indeed, is the idea of the pagoda architecture, of the
terrace architecture, of the bizarre constructions which
rise with projecting buttresses, rows of pillars, recesses, battlements, esplanades, and low walls, hanging gardens, and truncated pinnacles. It is a city, but a city
of the imagination. In many pages I could tell what
I saw in one day's lounging for a mile or so along the
edge of the precipice. The view changed at every
step, and was never half an hour the same in one
place. Nor did it need much fancy to create illusions
or pictures of unearthly beauty. There was a castle,
terraced up with columns, plain enough, and below it
a parade-ground; at any moment the knights in armor
and with banners might emerge from the red gates
and deploy there, while the ladies looked down from
the balconies. But there were many castles and fortresses and barracks and noble mansions. And the
rich sculpture in this brilliant color! In time I began to see queer details: a Richardson house, with
low portals and round arches, surmounted by a Nu-
remberg gable; perfect panels, 600 feet high, for the
setting of pictures; a train of cars partly derailed at
the door of a long, low warehouse, with a garden in
front of it. There was no end to such devices.

It was long before I could comprehend the vastness of the view, see the enormous chasms and rents
and seams, and the many architectural ranges separated by great gulfs, between me and the wall of the
mesa twelve miles distant. Away to the north-east
was the blue Navajo Mountain, the lone peak in the
horizon; but on the southern side of it lay a desert
level, which in the afternoon light took on the exact

appearance of a blue lake; its edge this side was a
wall thousands of feet high, many miles in length,
and straightly horizontal; over this seemed to fall
water. I could see the foam of it at the foot of the
cliff; and below that was a lake of shimmering silver,
in which the giant precipice and the fall and their
color were mirrored. Of course there was no silver
lake, and the reflection that simulated it was only
the sun on the lower part of the immense wall.

Some one said that all that was needed to perfect
this scene was a Niagara Falls. I thought what figure
a fall 150 feet high and 3000 long would make in this
arena. It would need a spy-glass to discover it. An
adequate Niagara here should be at least three miles
in breadth, and fall 2000 feet over one of these walls.
And the Yosemite—ah! the lovely Yosemite! Dump-
ed down into this wilderness of gorges and mountains,
it would take a guide who knew of its existence a
long time to find it.

The process of creation is here laid bare through
the geologic periods. The strata of rock, deposited
or upheaved, preserve their horizontal and parallel
courses. If we imagine a river flowing on a plain, it
would wear for itself a deeper and deeper channel.
The walls of this channel would recede irregularly by
weathering and by the coming in of other streams.
The channel would go on deepening, and the outer
walls would again recede. If the rocks were of different material and degrees of hardness, the forms
would be carved in the fantastic and architectural
manner we find them here. The Colorado flows
through the tortuous inner chasm, and where we see
it, it is 6000 feet below the surface where we stand,

and below the towers of the terraced forms nearer it.
The splendid views of the cañon at this point given
in Captain Dutton's report are from Point Sublime,
on the north side. There seems to have been no
way of reaching the river from that point. From the
south side the descent, though wearisome, is feasible.
It reverses mountaineering to descend 6000 feet for a
view, and there is a certain pleasure in standing on a
mountain summit without the trouble of climbing it.
Hance, the guide, who has charge of the well, has
made a path to the bottom. The route is seven miles
long. Half-way down he has a house by a spring.
At the bottom, somewhere in those depths, is a sort
of farm, grass capable of sustaining horses and cattle,
and ground where fruit-trees can grow. Horses are
actually living there, and parties descend there with
tents, and camp for days at a time. It is a world of
its own. Some of the photographic views presented
here, all inadequate, are taken from points on Hance's
trail. But no camera or pen can convey an adequate
conception of what Captain Dutton happily calls a
great innovation in the modern ideas of scenery. To
the eye educated to any other, it may be shocking,
grotesque, incomprehensible; but "those who have
long and carefully studied the Grand Cañon of the
Colorado do not hesitate for a moment to pronounce
it by far the most sublime of all earthly spectacles."

I have space only to refer to the geologic history
in Captain Dutton's report of 1882, of which there
should be a popular edition. The waters of the Atlantic once overflowed this region, and were separated
from the Pacific, if at all, only by a ridge. The story
is of long eras of deposits, of removal, of upheaval,

and of volcanic action. It is estimated that in one
period the thickness of strata removed and trans-
ported away was 10,000 feet. Long after the Colorado began its work of corrosion there was a mighty
upheaval. The reader will find the story of the making of the Grand Cañon more fascinating than any
romance.

Without knowing this story the impression that
one has in looking on this scene is that of immense
antiquity, hardly anywhere else on earth so overwhelming as here. It has been here in all its lonely
grandeur and transcendent beauty, exactly as it is, for
what to us is an eternity, unknown, unseen by human
eye. To the recent Indian, who roved along its brink
or descended to its recesses, it was not strange, because he had known no other than the plateau scenery. It is only within a quarter of a century that the
Grand Cañon has been known to the civilized world.
It is scarcely known now. It is a world largely unex-
plored. Those who best know it are most sensitive to
its awe and splendor. It is never twice the same, for,
as I said, it has an atmosphere of its own. I was
told by Hance that he once saw a thunder-storm in
it. He described the chaos of clouds in the pit, the
roar of the tempest, the reverberations of thunder, the
inconceivable splendor of the rainbows mingled with
the colors of the towers and terraces. It was as if
the world were breaking up. He fled away to his hut
in terror.

The day is near when this scenery must be made
accessible. A railway can easily be built from Flagstaff. The projected road from Utah, crossing the
Colorado at Lee's Ferry, would come within twenty

miles of the Grand Cañon, and a branch to it could
be built. The region is arid, and in the "sight-seeing"
part of the year the few surface wells and springs are
likely to go dry. The greatest difficulty would be in
procuring water for railway service or for such houses
of entertainment as are necessary. It could, no doubt,
be piped from the San Francisco Mountain. At any
rate, ingenuity will overcome the difficulties, and trav-
ellers from the wide world will flock thither, for there
is revealed the long-kept secret, the unique achieve-
ment of nature.

APPENDIX.

A CLIMATE FOR INVALIDS.

THE following notes on the climate of Southern California, written by Dr. H. A. Johnson, of Chicago, at the solicitation of the writer of this volume and for his information, I print with his permission, because the testimony of a physician who has made a special study of climatology in Europe and America, and is a recognized authority, belongs of right to the public:

The choice of a climate for invalids or semi-invalids involves the consideration of: First, the invalid, his physical condition (that is, disease), his peculiarities (mental and emotional), his social habits, and his natural and artificial needs. Second, the elements of climate, such as temperature, moisture, direction and force of winds, the averages of the elements, the extremes of variation, and the rapidity of change.

The climates of the western and south-western portions of the United States are well suited to a variety of morbid conditions, especially those pertaining to the pulmonary organs and the nervous system. Very few localities, however, are equally well adapted to diseases of innervation of circulation and respiration. For the first and second, as a rule, high altitudes are not advisable; for the third, altitudes of from two thousand to six thousand feet are not only admissible but by many thought to be desirable. It seems, however, probable that it is to the dryness of the air and the general antagonisms to vegetable growths, rather than to altitude alone, that the benefits derived in these regions by persons suffering from consumption and kindred diseases should be credited.

Proximity to large bodies of water, river valleys, and damp plateaus are undesirable as places of residence for invalids with lung troubles. There are exceptions to this rule. Localities near the sea with a climate subject to slight variations in temperature, a dry atmosphere, little rainfall, much sunshine, not so cold in winter as to prevent much out-door life and not so hot in summer as to make out-door exercise exhausting, are well adapted not only to troubles of the nervous and circulatory systems, but also to those of the respiratory organs.

Such a climate is found in the extreme southern portions of California. At San Diego the rainfall is much less, the air is drier, and the number of sunshiny days very much larger than on our Atlantic seaboard, or in Central and Northern California. The winters are not cold; flowers bloom in the open air all the year round; the summers are not hot. The mountains and sea combine to give to this region a climate with few sudden changes, and with a comfortable range of all essential elements.

A residence during a part of the winter of 1889–90 at Coronado Beach, and a somewhat careful study of the comparative climatology of the southwestern portions of the United States, leads me to think that we have few localities where the comforts of life can be secured, and which at the same time are so well adapted to the needs of a variety of invalids, as San Diego and its surroundings. In saying this I do not wish to be understood as preferring it to all others for some one condition or disease, but only that for weak hearts, disabled lungs, and worn-out nerves it seems to me to be unsurpassed.

CHICAGO, *July* 12, 1890.

THE COMING OF WINTER IN SOUTHERN CALIFORNIA.

From Mr. Theodore S. Van Dyke's altogether admirable book on *Southern California* I have permission to quote the following exquisite description of the floral procession from December to March, when the Land of the Sun is awakened by the first winter rain :

Sometimes this season commences with a fair rain in November, after a light shower or two in October, but some of the very best seasons begin about the time that all begin to lose hope. November adds its full tribute to the stream of sunshine that for months has poured along the land ; and, perhaps, December closes the long file of cloudless days with banners of blue and gold. The plains and slopes lie bare and brown; the low hills that break away from them are yellow with dead foxtail or wild oats, gray with mustard-stalks, or ashy green with chemisal or sage. Even the chaparral, that robes the higher hills in living green, has a tired air, and the long timber-line that marks the cañon winding up the mountain-slopes is decidedly paler. The sea-breeze has fallen off to a faint breath of air; the land lies silent and dreamy with golden haze; the air grows drier, the sun hotter, and the shade cooler; the smoke of brush-fires hangs at times along the sky; the water has risen in the springs and sloughs as if to meet the coming rain, but it has never looked less like rain than it now does.

Suddenly a new wind arises from the vast watery plains upon the south-west; long, fleecy streams of cloud reach out along the sky; the distant mountain-tops seem swimming in a film of haze, and the great California weather prophet—a creature upon whom the storms of adverse experience have beaten for years without making even a weather crack in the smooth cheek of his conceit—lavishes his wisdom as confidently as if he had never made a false prediction. After a large amount of fuss, and enough preliminary skirmishing over the sky for a dozen storms in any Eastern State, the clouds at last get ready, and a soft pattering is heard upon the roof—the sweetest music that ever cheers a Californian ear, and one which the author of "The Rain upon the Roof" should have heard before writing his poem.

When the sun again appears it is with a softer, milder beam than before. The land looks bright and refreshed, like a tired and dirty boy who has had a good bath and a nap, and already the lately bare plains and hillsides show a greenish tinge. Fine little leaves of various kinds are springing from the ground, but nearly all are lost in a general profusion of dark green ones, of such shape and delicacy of texture that a careless eye might readily take them for ferns. This is the alfileria, the prevailing flower of the land. The rain may continue at intervals. Daily the land grows greener, while the shades of green, varied by the play of sunlight on the slopes and rolling hills, increase in number and intensity. Here the color is soft, and there bright; yonder it rolls in wavy alternations, and yonder it reaches in an unbroken shade where the plain sweeps broad and free. For many weeks green is the only color, though cold nights may perhaps tinge it with a rusty red. About the first of February a little starlike flower of bluish pink begins to shine along the ground. This is the bloom of the alfileria, and swiftly it spreads from the southern slopes, where it begins, and runs from meadow to hill-top. Soon after a cream-colored bell-flower begins to nod from a tall, slender stalk; another of sky-blue soon opens beside it; beneath these a little five-petaled flower of deep pink tries to outshine the blossoms of the alfileria; and above them soon stands the radiant shooting-star, with reflexed petals of white, yellow, and pink shining behind its purplish ovaries. On every side violets, here of the purest golden hue and overpowering fragrance, appear in numbers beyond all conception. And soon six or seven varieties of clover, all with fine, delicate leaves, unfold flowers of yellow, red, and pink. Delicate little crucifers of white and yellow shine modestly below all these; little cream-colored flowers on slender scapes look skyward on every side; while others of purer white, with every variety of petal, crowd up among them. Standing now upon some hill-side that commands miles of landscape, one is dazzled with a blaze of color, from acres and acres of pink, great fields of violets, vast reaches of blue, endless sweeps of white.

Upon this—merely the warp of the carpet about to cover the land—the sun fast weaves a woof of splendor. Along the southern slopes of the lower hills soon beams the orange light of the poppy, which swiftly kindles the adjacent slopes, then flames along the meadow, and blazes upon the northern hill-sides. Spires of green, mounting on every side, soon open upon the top into lilies of deep lavender, and the scarlet bracts of the painted-cup glow side by side with the crimson of the cardinal-flower. And soon comes the iris, with its broad golden eye fringed with rays of lavender blue; and five varieties of phacelia overwhelm some places with waves of purple, blue, indigo, and whitish pink. The evening primrose covers the lower slopes with long sheets of brightest yellow, and from the hills above the rock-rose adds its golden bloom to that of the sorrel and the wild alfalfa, until the hills almost outshine the bright light from the slopes and plains. And through all this nods a tulip of most delicate lavender; vetches, lupins, and all the members of the wild-pea family are pushing and winding their way everywhere in every shade of crimson, purple, and white; along the ground crowfoot weaves a mantle of white, through which, amid a thousand comrades, the orthocarpus rears its tufted head of pink. Among all these are mixed a thousand other flowers, plenty enough as plenty would be accounted in other countries, but here mere pin-points on a great map of colors.

As the stranger gazes upon this carpet that now covers hill and dale, undulates over the table-lands, and robes even the mountain with a brilliancy and breadth of color that strikes the eye from miles away, he exhausts his vocabulary of superlatives, and goes away imagining he has seen it all. Yet he has seen only the background of an embroidery more varied, more curious and splendid, than the carpet upon which it is wrought. Asters bright with centre of gold and lavender rays soon shine high above the iris, and a new and larger tulip of deepest yellow nods where its lavender cousin is drooping its lately proud head. New bell-flowers of white and blue and indigo rise above the first, which served merely as ushers to the display, and whole acres ablaze with the orange of the poppy are fast turning with the indigo of the larkspur. Where the ground was lately aglow with the marigold and the four-o'clock the tall penstemon now reaches out a hundred arms full-hung with trumpets of purple and pink. Here the silene rears high its head with fringed corolla of scarlet; and there the wild gooseberry dazzles the eye with a perfect shower of tubular flowers of the same bright color. The mimulus alone is almost enough to color the hills. Half a dozen varieties, some with long, narrow, trumpet-shaped flowers, others with broad flaring mouths; some of them tall herbs, and others large shrubs, with varying shades of dark red, light red, orange, cream-color, and yellow, spangle hill-side, rock-pile, and ravine. Among them the morning-glory twines with flowers of purest white, new lupins climb over the old ones, and the trailing vetch festoons rock and shrub and tree with long garlands of crimson, purple, and pink. Over the scarlet of the gooseberry or the gold of the high-bush mimulus along the hills, the honeysuckle hangs its tubes of richest cream-color, and the wild cucumber pours a shower of white over the green leaves of the sumach or sage. Snap-dragons of blue and white, dandelions that you must look at three or four times to be certain what they are, thistles that are soft and tender with flowers too pretty for the thistle family, orchids that you may try in vain to classify, and sages and mints of which you can barely recognize the genera, with cruciferæ, compositæ, and what-not, add to the glare and confusion.

Meanwhile, the chaparral, which during the long dry season has robed the hills in sombre green, begins to brighten with new life; new leaves adorn the ragged red arms of the manzanita, and among them blow thousands of little urn-shaped flowers of rose-color and white. The bright green of one lilac is almost lost in a luxuriance of sky-blue blossoms, and the white lilac looks at a distance as if drifted over with snow. The cercocarpus almost rivals the lilac in its display of white and blue, and the dark, forbidding adenostoma now showers forth dense panicles of little white flowers. Here, too, a new mimulus pours floods of yellow light, and high above them all the yucca rears its great plume of purple and white.

Thus marches on for weeks the floral procession, new turns bringing new banners into view, or casting on old ones a brighter light, but ever showing a riotous profusion of splendor until member after member drops gradually out of the ranks, and only a band of stragglers is left marching away into the summer. But myriads of ferns, twenty-one varieties of which are quite common, and of a fineness and delicacy rarely seen elsewhere, still stand green in the shade of the rocks and trees along the hills, and many a flower lingers in the timber or cañons long after its friends on the open hills or plains have faded away. In the cañons and timber are also many flowers that are not found in the open ground, and as late as the middle of September, only twenty miles from the sea, and at an elevation of but fifteen hundred feet, I have gathered bouquets that would attract immediate attention anywhere. The whole land abounds with flowers both curious and lovely; but those only have been mentioned which force themselves upon one's attention. Where the sheep have not ruined all beauty, and the rains have been sufficient, they take as full possession of the land as the daisy and wild carrot do of some Eastern meadows. There are thousands of others, which it would be a hopeless task to enumerate, which are even more numerous than most of the favorite wild flowers are in the East, yet they are not abundant enough to give character to the country. For instance, there is a great larkspur, six feet high, with a score of branching arms, all studded with spurred flowers of such brilliant red that it looks like a fountain of strontium fire; but you will not see it every time you turn around. A tall lily grows in the same way, with a hundred golden flowers shining on its many arms, but it must be sought in certain places. So the tiger-lily and the columbine must be sought in the mountains, the rose and sweetbrier on low ground, the night-shades and the helianthus in the timbered cañons and gulches.

Delicacy and brilliancy characterize nearly all the California flowers, and nearly all are so strange, so different from the other members of their families, that they would be an ornament to any greenhouse. The alfileria, for instance, is the richest and strongest fodder in the world. It is the main-stay of the stock-grower, and when raked up after drying makes excellent hay; yet it is a geranium, delicate and pretty, when not too rank.

But suddenly the full blaze of color is gone, and the summer is at hand. Brown tints begin to creep over the plains; the wild oats no longer ripple in silvery waves beneath the sun and wind; and the foxtail, that shone so brightly green along the hill-side, takes on a golden hue. The light lavender tint of the chorizanthe now spreads along the hills where the poppy so lately flamed, and over the dead morning-glory the dodder weaves its orange floss. A vast army of cruciferæ and compositæ soon overruns the land with bright yellow, and numerous varieties of mint tinge it with blue or purple; but the greater portion of the annual vegetation is dead or dying. The distant peaks of granite now begin to glow at evening with a soft purple hue; the light poured into the deep ravines towards sundown floods them with a crimson mist; on the shady hill-sides the chaparral looks bluer, and on the sunny hill-sides is a brighter green than before.

COMPARATIVE TEMPERATURE AROUND THE WORLD.

The following table, published by the Pasadena Board of Trade, shows the comparative temperature of well-known places in various parts of the world, arranged according to the difference between their average winter and average summer:

PLACE.	Winter.	Spring.	Summer.	Autumn.	Difference Summer, Winter.
Funchal, Madeira..............	62.88	64.55	70.89	70.19	8.01
St. Michael, Azores............	57.83	61.17	68.33	62.33	10.50
PASADENA...................	56.00	61.07	67.61	62.31	11.61
Santa Cruz, Canaries..........	64.65	68.87	76.68	74.17	12.03
Santa Barbara................	54.29	59.45	67.71	65.11	13.42
Nassau, Bahama Islands.......	70.67	77.67	86.00	80.33	15.33
San Diego, California..........	54.09	60.14	69.67	64.65	15.58
Cadiz, Spain.................	52.90	59.93	70.43	65.55	17.53
Lisbon, Portugal..............	53.00	60.00	71.00	62.00	18.00
Malta......................	57.46	62.76	78.20	71.03	20.74
Algiers.....................	55.00	66.00	77.00	60.00	22.00
St. Augustine, Florida........	58.25	68.69	80.36	71.90	22.11
Rome, Italy.................	48.90	57.65	72.16	65.96	23.26
Sacramento, California........	47.92	59.17	71.19	61.72	23.27
Mentone....................	49.50	60.00	73.00	56.00	23.50
Nice, Italy..................	47.88	56.23	72.26	61.65	24.44
New Orleans, Louisiana.......	56.00	69.37	81.08	69.80	25.08
Cairo, Egypt................	58.52	73.58	85.10	71.48	26.58
Jacksonville, Florida..........	55.02	68.88	81.95	62.51	26.91
Pau, France.................	41.86	54.06	70.72	57.39	28.86
Florence, Italy...............	44.30	56.00	74.00	60.70	29.70
San Antonio, Texas...........	52.74	70.48	83.73	71.56	30.99
Aiken, South Carolina.........	45.82	61.32	77.36	61.96	31.54
Fort Yuma, California	57.96	73.40	92.07	75.66	34.11
Visalia, California............	45.38	59.40	80.78	60.34	35.40
Santa Fé, New Mexico........	30.28	50.06	70.50	51.34	40.22
Boston, Mass................	28.08	45.61	68.68	51.04	40.60
New York, N. Y..............	31.93	48.26	72.62	48.50	40.69
Albuquerque, New Mexico.....	34.78	56.56	76.27	56.33	41.40
Denver, Colorado.............	27.66	46.33	71.66	47.16	44.00
St. Paul, Minnesota...........	15.09	41.29	68.03	44.98	52.94
Minneapolis, Minnesota........	12.87	40.12	68.34	45.33	55.47

CALIFORNIA AND ITALY.

The Los Angeles Chamber of Commerce, in its pamphlet describing that city and county, gives a letter from the Signal Service Observer at Sacramento, comparing the temperature of places in California and Italy. He writes:

To prove to your many and intelligent readers the equability and uniformity of the climate of Santa Barbara, San Diego, and Los Angeles, as compared with Mentone and San Remo, of the Riviera of Italy and of Corfu, I append the monthly temperature for each place. Please notice a much warmer temperature in winter at the California stations, and also a much cooler summer temperature at the same places than at any of the foreign places, except Corfu. The table speaks with more emphasis and certainty than I can, and is as follows:

Month	San Diego's mean temperature	Santa Barbara's mean temperature	Los Angeles' mean temperature	Mentone's mean temperature	San Remo's mean temperature	Corfu's mean temperature
January	55.7	54.4	52.8	48.2	47.2	55.6
February	54.2	55.6	54.2	48.5	50.2	51.8
March	55.6	56.4	56.0	52.0	52.0	55.6
April	57.8	58.8	57.9	57.2	57.0	58.3
May	61.1	60.2	61.0	63.0	62.9	66.7
June	64.4	62.6	55.5	70.0	69.2	72.3
July	67.3	65.7	68.3	75.0	74.3	67.7
August	68.7	67.0	69.5	75.0	73.8	81.3
September	66.6	65.6	67.5	69.0	70.6	78.8
October	62.5	62.1	62.7	71.4	61.8	70.8
November	58.2	58.0	58.8	54.0	58.3	63.8
December	55.5	55.3	51.8	49.0	49.3	58.4
Averages	60.6	60.2	60.4	60.4	60.1	65.6

The table on pages 210 and 211, " Extremes of Heat and Cold," is published by the San Diego Land and Farm Company, whose pamphlet says:

The United States records at San Diego Signal Station show that in ten years there were but 120 days on which the mercury passed 80°. Of these 120 there were but 41 on which it passed 85°, but 22 when it passed 90°, but four over 95°, and only one over 100°: to wit, 101°, the highest ever recorded here. During all this time there was not a day on which the mercury did not fall to at least 70° during the night, and there were but five days on which it did not fall even lower. During the same ten years there were but six days on which the mercury fell below 35°. This low temperature comes only in extremely dry weather in winter, and lasts but a few minutes, happening just before sunrise. On two of these six days it fell to 32° at daylight, the lowest point ever registered here. The lowest mid-day temperature is 52°, occurring only four times in these ten years. From 65° to 70° is the average temperature of noonday throughout the greater part of the year.

FIVE YEARS IN SANTA BARBARA.

The following table, from the self-registering thermometer in the observatory of Mr. Hugh D. Vail, shows the mean temperature of each month in the years 1885 to 1889 at Santa Barbara, and also the mean temperature of the warmest and coldest days in each month:

Month	1885			1886			1887			1888			1889			
	Mean Temperature of each Month	Mean Temperature of Warmest Day	Mean Temperature of Coldest Day	Mean Temperature of each Month	Mean Temperature of Warmest Day	Mean Temperature of Coldest Day	Mean Temperature of each Month	Mean Temperature of Warmest Day	Mean Temperature of Coldest Day	Mean Temperature of each Month	Mean Temperature of Warmest Day	Mean Temperature of Coldest Day	Mean Temperature of each Month	Mean Temperature of Warmest Day	Mean Temperature of Coldest Day	Monthly Rainfall, Inches.
January	53.2	57.0	49.5	53.9	73.5	47.5	51.67	62.5	49.0	49.0	58.7	41.0	53.0	58.0	48.8	0.99
February	56.7	65.5	51.5	59.6	70.0	45.0	50.4	61.1	45.5	53.8	57.5	49.0	54.1	65.0	45.8	1.29
March	59.1	62.5	50.0	55.1	59.5	46.2	57.0	62.8	52.0	55.0	60.5	46.0	58.0	67.0	52.5	7.51
April	60.9	70.5	54.0	55.7	61.5	50.5	58.43	66.8	51.0	59.9	73.0	51.7	59.9	72.7	52.7	0.49
May	60.0	64.6	54.0	60.5	65.5	51.0	60.0	67.0	55.3	57.6	69.0	59.5	60.0	68.5	54.5	0.76
June	62.0	68.0	58.5	62.0	67.5	56.5	63.7	79.0	59.0	61.4	73.5	59.5	62.5	65.7	58.5	0.13
July	66.1	74.0	62.2	72.0	79.0	63.8	71.3	71.3	62.0	73.2	79.0	79.0	64.2	84.0	61.0	....
August	68.0	76.0	61.5	66.8	72.0	63.3	64.6	69.9	63.9	66.3	72.0	68.0	67.2	77.0	62.0	....
September	66.9	78.8	62.5	65.8	68.3	62.2	66.0	69.1	62.0	67.9	76.2	63.5	67.2	78.0	62.0	....
October	62.9	72.0	58.3	62.5	62.5	51.7	63.3	74.0	61.5	63.3	76.9	63.2	68.8	70.3	60.0	8.89
November	58.9	64.8	50.0	56.2	66.5	49.8	58.9	63.5	57.5	59.8	61.5	51.5	59.6	63.7	34.5	8.21
December	57.9	63.7	52.0	55.8	65.8	49.5	52.8	59.6	49.0	54.5	63.0	52.0	54.4	69.7	50.0	10.64

14

Observations made at San Diego City, compiled from Report of the Chief Signal Officer of the U. S. Army.

MONTH.	Average number of cloudy days for each month and year.	Average number of fair days for each month and year.	Average number of clear days for each month and year.	Average cloudiness, scale 0 to 10, for each month and year.	Average hourly velocity of wind for each month and year.	Average precipitation for each month and year.	Minimum temperature for each month and year.	Maximum temperature for each month and year.	Mean temperature for each month and year.	Mean normal barometer of San Diego for each month and year for four years.
January	8.5	11.2	11.3	4.1	5.1	1.85	32.0	78.0	53.6	30.027
February	7.9	11.3	9.0	4.4	6.0	2.07	35.0	82.6	54.3	30.058
March	9.6	12.7	8.7	4.8	6.4	0.97	38.0	99.0	55.7	30.004
April	7.9	11.9	10.2	4.4	6.6	0.68	39.0	87.0	57.7	29.965
May	10.9	12.1	8.0	5.2	6.7	0.26	45.4	94.0	61.0	29.893
June	8.1	15.2	6.7	5.0	6.3	0.05	51.0	94.0	64.4	29.864
July	6.7	16.4	8.2	4.7	6.3	0.02	54.0	86.0	67.1	29.849
August	7.7	16.9	9.4	4.1	6.0	0.23	54.0	86.0	68.7	29.894
September	4.4	13.9	11.7	3.7	5.9	0.05	49.5	101.0	66.8	29.840
October	5.6	12.6	12.8	3.9	5.4	0.49	44.0	92.0	62.9	29.905
November	6.5	10.0	13.5	3.6	5.1	0.70	38.0	85.0	58.3	29.991
December	6.6	11.2	13.2	3.7	5.1	2.12	32.0	82.0	55.6	30.009
Mean annual.	87.4	155.1	122.7	4.3	5.9	9.49	42.6	88.8	60.5	29.942

EXTREMES OF HEAT AND COLD.

The following table, taken from the Report of the Chief Signal Officer, shows the highest and lowest temperatures recorded since the opening of stations of the Signal Service at the points named, for the number of years indicated. An asterisk (*) denotes below zero:

LOCALITY OF STATION.	No. of Years of Observation.	JAN.		FEB.		MARCH.		APRIL.		MAY.		JUNE.	
		Maximum.	Minimum.	Maximum.	Minimum.	Maximum.	Minimum.	Maximum.	Minimum.	Maximum.	Minimum.	Maximum.	Minimum.
Charleston, S. C.	12	80	23	78	26	85	28	87	32	94	17	94	65
Denver, Col.	12	67	*29	72	*22	81	*10	83	4	92	27	89	50
Jacksonville, Fla.	12	80	24	83	32	88	31	91	37	99	48	101	62
L'S ANGELES, CAL.	6	82	30	86	28	99	34	94	39	100	40	104	47
New Orleans, La.	13	78	20	80	33	84	37	86	38	92	56	97	65
Newport, R. I.	2	48	2	50	4	60	4	62	26	75	33	91	41
New York.	13	64	*6	69	*4	72	*3	81	20	94	34	95	47
Pensacola, Fla.	4	74	29	78	31	79	36	87	34	93	47	97	64
SAN DIEGO, CAL.	12	78	32	83	35	99	38	87	39	91	45	94	51
San Francisco, Cal.	12	69	36	71	35	77	39	81	40	86	45	95	48

EXTREMES OF HEAT AND COLD.—*Continued.*

LOCALITY OF STATION	No. of Years of Observation.	JULY.		AUG.		SEPT.		OCT.		NOV.		DEC.	
		Maximum.	Minimum.	Maximum.	Minimum.	Maximum.	Minimum.	Maximum.	Minimum.	Maximum.	Minimum.	Maximum.	Minimum.
Charleston, S. C....	12	94	69	96	69	94	64	89	49	81	33	78	22
Denver, Col......	12	94	59	93	60	93	51	84	38	73	23	69	1
Jacksonville, Fla....	12	104	68	100	66	98	56	92	40	84	30	81	19
L'S ANG'LES, CAL.	6	98	51	100	50	104	44	97	43	86	34	88	30
New Orleans, La...	13	96	70	97	69	92	58	89	40	82	32	78	20
Newport, R. I......	2	87	56	85	45	77	39	75	29	62	17	56	89
New York........	13	99	57	96	53	100	36	83	31	74	7	66	96
Pensacola, Fla.....	4	97	64	93	69	93	57	89	45	81	28	76	17
SAN DIEGO, CAL.	12	86	54	86	54	101	50	92	44	85	38	82	32
San Francisco, Cal..	12	83	49	89	50	92	50	84	45	78	41	68	34

STATEMENTS OF SMALL CROPS.

The following statements of crops on small pieces of ground, mostly in Los Angeles County, in 1890, were furnished to the Chamber of Commerce in Los Angeles, and are entirely trustworthy. Nearly all of them bear date August 1st. This is a fair sample from all Southern California :

PEACHES.

Ernest Dewey, Pomona—Golden Cling Peaches, 10 acres, 7 years old, produced 47 tons green ; sold dried for $4800 ; cost of production, $243.70 ; net profit, $4556.30. Soil, sandy loam ; not irrigated. Amount of rain, 28 inches, winter of 1889–90.

H. H. Rose, Santa Anita Township (¾ of a mile from Lamanda Park)—2⅔ acres ; produced 47,543 pounds ; sold for $863.46 ; cost of production, $104 ; net profit, $759.46. Soil, light sandy loam ; not irrigated. Produced in 1889 12,000 pounds, which sold at $1.70 per 100 pounds.

E. R. Thompson, Azusa (2 miles south of depot)—2½ acres, 233 trees, produced 57,655 pounds ; sold for $864.82½ ; cost of production, $140 ; net profit, $724.82½. Soil, sandy loam ; irrigated three times in summer. 1 inch to 7 acres. Trees 7 years old, not more than two-thirds grown.

P. O'Connor, Downey—20 trees produced 4000 pounds ; sold for $60 ; cost of production $5 ; net profit, $55. Soil, sandy loam ; not irrigated. Crop sold on the ground.

H. Hood, Downey City (¼ of a mile from depot)—¼ of an acre produced

7½ tons; sold for $150; cost of production, $10; net profit, $140. Damp sandy soil; not irrigated.

F. D. Smith (between Azusa and Glendora, 1¼ miles from depot)—1 acre produced 14,361 pounds; sold for $252.51; cost of production, $20; net profit, $232.51. Dark sandy loam; irrigated once. Trees 5 and 6 years old.

P. O. Johnson, Ranchito—17 trees, 10 years old, produced 4½ tons; sold 4¼ tons for $120; cost of production, $10; net profit, $110; very little irrigation. Sales were ¼c. per pound under market rate.

<h2 style="text-align:center">PRUNES.</h2>

E. P. Naylor (3 miles from Pomona)—15 acres produced 149 tons; sold for $7450; cost of production, $527; net profit, $6923. Soil, loam, with some sand; irrigated, 1 inch per 10 acres.

W. H. Baker, Downey (½ of a mile from depot)—1½ acres produced 12,529 pounds; sold for $551.90; cost of production, $50; net profit, $501.90. Soil, sandy loam; not irrigated.

Howe Bros. (2 miles from Lordsburg)—800 trees, which had received no care for 2 years, produced 28 tons; sold for $1400; cost of production, $200; net profit, $1200. Soil, gravelly loam, red; partially irrigated. Messrs. Howe state that they came into possession of this place in March, 1890. The weeds were as high as the trees and the ground was very hard. Only about 500 of the trees had a fair crop on them.

W. A. Spalding, Azusa—⅛ of an acre produced 10,404 pounds; sold for $156.06; cost of production, $10; net profit, $146.06. Soil, sandy loam.

E. A. Hubbard, Pomona (1½ miles from depot)—4½ acres produced 24 tons; sold green for $1080; cost of production, $280; net profit, $800. Soil, dark sandy loam; irrigated. This entire ranch of 9 acres was bought in 1884 for $1575.

F. M. Smith (1¼ miles east of Azusa)—⅔ of an acre produced 17,174 pounds; sold for $315.84; cost of production, $25; net profit, $290. Soil, deep, dark sandy loam; irrigated once in the spring. Trees 5 years old.

George Rhorer (¼ of a mile east of North Pomona)—13 acres produced 88 tons; sold for $4400 on the trees; cost of production, $260; net profit, $4140. Soil, gravelly loam; irrigated, 1 inch to 8 acres. Trees planted 5 years ago last spring.

J. S. Flory (between the Big and Little Tejunga rivers)—1¼ acres or 135 trees 20 feet apart each way; 100 of the trees 4 years old, the balance of the trees 5 years old; produced 5230 pounds dried; sold for $523; cost of production, $18; net profit, $505. Soil, light loam, with some sand; not irrigated.

W. Caruthers (2 miles north of Downey)—¾ of an acre produced 5 tons; sold for $222; cost of production, $7.50; net profit, $215. Soil, sandy loam; not irrigated. Trees 4 years old.

James Loney, Pomona—2 acres; product sold for $1150; cost of production, $50; net profit, $1100. Soil, sandy loam.

I. W. Lord, Eswena—5 acres produced 40 tons; sold for $2000; cost of production, $300; net profit, $1700. Soil, sandy loam.

M. B. Moulton, Pomona—3 acres; sold for $1873; cost of production, $215; net profit, $1658. Soil, deep sandy loam. Trees 9 years old.

Ernest Dewey, Pomona—6 acres produced 38 tons green; dried, at 10 cents a pound, $3147; cost of production, $403; profit, $2734. Soil, sandy loam; irrigated one inch to 10 acres. Sixty per cent. increase over former year.

C. S. Ambrose, Pomona—12 acres produced 77 tons; $50 per ton gross, $3850; labor of one hand one year, $150; profit, $3700. Soil, gravelly; very little irrigation. Prunes sold on trees.

ORANGES.

Joachim F. Jarchow, San Gabriel—2½ acres; 10-year trees; product sold for $1650; cost of production $100, including cultivation of 7½ acres, not bearing; net profit, $1550.

F. D. Smith, Azusa—6½ acres produced 600 boxes; sold for $1200; cost of production, $130; net profit, $1070. Soil, dark sandy loam; irrigated three times. Trees 4 years old.

George Lightfoot, South Pasadena—5½ acres produced 700 boxes; sold for $1100; cost of production, $50; net profit, $1050. Soil, rich, sandy loam; irrigated once a year.

H. Hood, Downey—½ of an acre produced 275 boxes; sold for $275; cost of production, $25; net profit, $250. Soil, damp, sandy; not irrigated.

W. G. Earle, Azusa—1 acre produced 210 boxes; sold for $262; cost of production, $15; net profit, $247. Soil, sandy loam; irrigated four times.

Nathaniel Hayden, Vernon—4 acres; 986 boxes at $1.20 per box; sales, $1182; cost of production, $50; net profit, $1132. Loam; irrigated. Other products on the 4 acres.

H. O. Fosdick, Santa Ana—1 acre; 6 years old; 350 boxes; sales, $700; cost of production and packing, $50; net profit, $650. Loam; irrigated.

J. H. Isbell, Rivera—1 acre, 82 trees; 16 years old; sales, $600; cost of production, $25; profit, $575. Irrigated. $1.40 per box for early delivery, $1.65 for later.

GRAPES.

William Bernhard, Monte Vista—10 acres produced 25 tons; sold for $750; cost of production, $70; net profit, $680. Soil, heavy loam; not irrigated. Vines 5 years old.

Dillon, Kennealy & McClure, Burbank (1 mile from Roscoe Station)—200 acres produced 90,000 gallons of wine; cost of production, $5000; net profit, about $30,000. Soil, sandy loam; not irrigated; vineyard in very healthy condition.

P. O'Connor (2½ miles south of Downey)—12 acres produced 100 tons; sold for $1500; cost of production, $360; net profit, $1140. Soil, sandy loam; not irrigated. Vines planted in 1884, when the land would not sell for $100 per acre.

J. K. Banks (1¾ miles from Downey)—10 acres produced 250 tons; sold for $3900; cost of production, $1300; net profit, $2600. Soil, sandy loam.

BERRIES.

W. Y. Earle (2½ miles from Azusa)—Strawberries, 2½ acres produced 15,000 boxes; sold for $750; cost of production, $225; net profit, $525. Soil, sandy loam; irrigated. Shipped 3000 boxes to Ogden, Utah, and 6000 boxes to Albuquerque and El Paso.

Benjamin Norris, Pomona—Blackberries, ½ of an acre produced 2500 pounds; sold for $100; cost of production, $5; net profit, $95. Soil, light sandy; irrigated.

S. H. Eye, Covina—Raspberries, ⅗ of an acre produced 1800 pounds; sold for $195; cost of production, $85; net profit, $110. Soil, sandy loam; irrigated.

J. O. Houser, Covina—Blackberries, ¼ of an acre produced 648 pounds; sold for $71.28; cost of production, $18; net profit, $53.28. Soil, sandy loam; irrigated. First year's crop.

APRICOTS.

T. D. Leslie (1 mile from Pomona)—1 acre produced 10 tons; sold for $250; cost of production, $60; net profit, $190. Soil, loose, gravelly; irrigated; 1 inch to 10 acres. First crop.

George Lightfoot, South Pasadena—2 acres produced 11 tons; sold for $260; cost of production, $20; net profit, $240. Soil, sandy loam; not irrigated.

T. D. Smith, Azusa—1 acre produced 13,555 pounds; sold for $169.44; cost of production, $25; net profit, $144.44. Soil, sandy loam; irrigated once. Trees 5 years old.

W. Y. Earle (2½ miles from Azusa)—6 acres produced 6 tons; sold for $350; cost of production, $25; net profit, $325. Soil, sandy loam; not irrigated. Trees 3 years old.

W. A. Spalding, Azusa—335 trees produced 15,478 pounds; sold for $647.43; cost of production, $50; net profit, $597.43. Soil, sandy loam.

Mrs. Winkler, Pomona—¾ of an acre, 90 trees; product sold for $381; cost of production, $28.40; net profit, $352.60. Soil, sandy loam; not irrigated. Only help, small boys and girls.

MISCELLANEOUS FRUITS.

E. A. Bonine, Lamanda Park — Apricots, nectarines, prunes, peaches, and lemons, 30 acres produced 160 tons; sold for $8000; cost of production, $1500; net profit, $6500. No irrigation.

J. P. Fleming (1½ miles from Rivera)—Walnuts, 40 acres produced 12½ tons; sold for $2120; cost of production, $120; net profit, $2000. Soil, sandy loam; not irrigated.

George Lightfoot, South Pasadena — Lemons, 2 acres produced 500 boxes; sold for $720; cost of production, $20; net profit, $700. Soil, rich sandy loam; not irrigated. Trees 10 years old.

W. A. Spalding, Azusa—Nectarines, 96 trees produced 19,378 pounds; sold for $242.22; cost of production, $35; net profit, $207.22. Soil, sandy loam.

F. D. Smith, Azusa—Nectarines, 1½ acres produced 36,350 pounds; sold for $363.50; cost of production, $35; net profit, $318.50. Soil, deep dark sandy loam; irrigated once in spring. Trees 5 and 6 years old.

C. D. Ambrose (4 miles north of Pomona)—Pears, 3 acres produced 33,422 pounds; sold green for $1092.66; cost of production, $57; net profit, $1035.66. Soil, foot-hill loam; partly irrigated.

N. Hayden—Statement of amount of fruit taken from 4 acres for one season at Vernon District: 985 boxes oranges, 15 boxes lemons, 8000 pounds apricots, 2200 pounds peaches, 200 pounds loquats, 2500 pounds nectarines, 4000 pounds apples, 1000 pounds plums, 1000 pounds prunes, 1000 pounds figs, 150 pounds walnuts, 500 pounds pears. Proceeds, $1650. A family of five were supplied with all the fruit they wanted besides the above.

POTATOES.

O. Bullis, Compton—28¾ acres produced 3000 sacks; sold for $3000; cost of production, $500; net profit, $2500. Soil, peat; not irrigated. This land has been in potatoes 3 years, and will be sown to cabbages, thus producing two crops this year.

P. F. Cogswell, El Monte — 25 acres produced 150 tons; sold for $3400; cost of production, $450; net profit, $2950. Soil, sediment; not irrigated.

M. Metcalf, El Monte—8 acres produced 64 tons; sold for $900; cost of production, $50; net profit, $850. Soil, sandy loam; not irrigated.

Jacob Vernon (1½ miles from Covina)—3 acres produced 400 sacks; sold for $405.88; cost of production, $5; net profit, $400.88. Soil, sandy loam; irrigated one acre. Two-thirds of crop was volunteer.

H. Hood, Downey—Sweet potatoes, 1 acre produced 300 sacks; sold for $300; cost of production, $30; net profit, $270. Soil, sandy loam; not irrigated.

C. C. Stub, Savannah (1 mile from depot)—10 acres produced 1000 sacks; sold for $2000; cost of production, $100; net profit, $1900. Soil, sandy loam; not irrigated. A grain crop was raised on the same land this year.

ONIONS.

F. A. Atwater and C. P. Eldridge, Clearwater—1 acre produced 211 sacks; sold for $211; cost of production, $100; net profit, $111. Soil, sandy loam; no irrigation. At present prices the onions would have brought $633.

Charles Lauber, Downey—1 acre produced 113 sacks; sold for $642; cost of production, $50; net profit, $592. No attention was paid to the cultivation of this crop. Soil, sandy loam; not irrigated. At present prices the same onions would have brought $803.

MISCELLANEOUS VEGETABLES.

Eugene Lassene, University—Pumpkins, 5 acres produced 150 loads; sold for $4 per load; cost of production, $3 per acre; net profit, $585. Soil, sandy loam. A crop of barley was raised from the same land this year.

P. K. Wood, Clearwater — Pea-nuts, 3 acres produced 5000 pounds; sold for $250; cost of production, $40; net profit, $210. Soil, light sandy; not irrigated. Planted too deep, and got about one-third crop.

Oliver E. Roberts (Terrace Farm, Cahuenga Valley)—3 acres tomatoes; sold product for $461.75. Soil, foot-hill; not irrigated; second crop, watermelons. One-half acre green peppers; sold product for $54.30. 1½ acres of green peas; sold product for $220. 17 fig-trees; first crop sold for $40. Total product of 5¼ acres, $776.05.

Jacob Miller, Cahuenga—Green peas, 10 acres; 43,615 pounds; sales, $3052; cost of production and marketing, $500; profit, $2552. Soil, foot-hill; not irrigated. Second crop, melons.

W. W. Bliss, Duarte — Honey, 215 stands; 15,000 pounds; sales, 8785. Mountain district. Bees worth $1 to $3 per stand.

James Stewart, Downey—Figs, 3 acres; 20 tons, at $50, $1000. Not irrigated; 26 inches rain; 1 acre of trees 16 years old, 2 acres 5 years. Figs sold on trees.

The mineral wealth of Southern California is not yet appreciated. Among the rare minerals which promise much is a very large deposit of tin in the Temescal Cañon, below South Riverside. It is in the hands of an English company. It is estimated that there are 23 square miles rich in tin ore, and it is said that the average yield of tin is 20¼ per cent.

INDEX.

THE END.

www.ingramcontent.com/pod-product-compliance
Lightning Source LLC
Chambersburg PA
CBHW030102030726
47498CB00007B/2225